The Death Brothers:

A Supernatural Awakening

Contents

Introduction

Taken from the Bad Angel: Redemption

The Death Brothers

It was 1793 in a small village just outside of London, England. It was one hundred years before the first vampire slayer, Harold Caine, existed. One night, a tall ghostly figure wearing a long black robe hovered to the front stoop of a cottage. He looked in all directions before he reached inside his robe and pulled out a big thick leather-bound brown book. It was the Book of the Dead, and the home belonged to Stephen and Patrick Dupree.

Upon reading the book, they discovered their purpose in life. It spoke of their lineage and how it would survive through the years to battle the forces of evil. It just so happens that at the time, the evils the brothers faced were vampires and werewolves.

Stephen was the oldest, and his main occupation was hunting vampires. Patrick hunted werewolves. Back then, werewolves outnumbered vampires and spread across the globe. Patrick had hunted and killed most of the werewolves in Europe. So, after destroying a famed werewolf pack, Patrick suggested they needed

1

to take their gifts to the "New World." Because vampires were smarter and less careless, Stephen realized he'd destroyed enough of them in Europe and decided to join his brother in America.

Stephen was the bigger of the two and more muscular, about six-feet, seven inches tall. He had curly blond hair and was a former Sergeant in the Foreign Legion. Patrick was a few inches shorter, with brunette hair, slender, and a devout Christian. He was the more patient of the two.

The entire ship traveling to America was filled with supernatural creatures. There, they ran into Metalles, a powerful vampire. Metalles and his crew had killed Stephen in battle one night.

Patrick carried Stephen's body to a storage room below decks. He lay Stephen's body on a metal crate that mixed in with the luggage. He intended to burn Stephen's body so his brother wouldn't come back as part of the undead creatures they'd spent their lives hunting.

Patrick took Stephen's hand and squeezed. "I'm sorry, brother, that I failed you. I will avenge you, though."

Patrick cuffed Stephen's hand. He kissed it and brought it up to his forehead. *God, please take my brother into your bosom and make him feel welcomed in Heaven as he never felt on Earth.* He felt a wave of energy flow back and forth from his brother's hand to his. Stephen's body then sprang back to life.

On that night, the brothers realized that one of their combined gifts was that they were able to bring each other back from the dead. They eventually cleansed the ship of supernatural creatures before pulling into the Port of New York a few days later.

Amongst their other gifts, the brothers lived beyond their natural lifespans. Before they could die, their successors had to be found first. They'd use their skills and abilities, some supernatural, to truly earn the title of…the Death Brothers.

Part 1

An Old Score

New York City

It was three o'clock in the morning, and Central High School was closed. Red electricity flashed at the center of one of the three-science classrooms. Smoke engulfed the classroom. Ten science tables were in the class, five on each side: they were waist-high, rectangular, with black marble tops, wooden frames, and drawers. A metal sink was slightly to the right, with a J-shaped faucet attached. A tall figure in a black hooded robe appeared out of the smoke. It was the Hangman. He walked toward the center table to his right.

"The slayer and demon hunter are, no doubt, turning over every stone on earth to find me." The Hangman placed an old dirty leather bag on top of the table. "But with this spell, they'll be too preoccupied to be searching for me."

He lifted the flap of the pouch, which opened from the left

and over the top. He pulled out a small vial of blood from a bat; twigs from a tree branch in the Garden of Eden; fur from a werewolf; dirt from a cemetery; and blood from a dead human. He placed the items in the sink. He pointed his fist, which wore the Power Ring. It covered three fingers and had a ruby, green emerald, and white marble in the center. He fired a pink beam of light that struck the contents in the sink. An odorless pink smoke rose from the sink as the contents dissolved and disappeared.

The Hangman stretched out his arms to the side, and the wall of windows shattered. The pink smoke escaped the classroom and spread out into the sky over the vast city. He turned on the faucet to clear any residue in the sink.

Now hopefully, if she was telling the truth, this will bring to life some of the vilest creatures known to mankind. And will keep all those busy who wish to stand in my way and hinder my plans.

The Gulf of Mexico

Jericho sat on a wood crate on a tugboat that slowly sailed across the water. It was dark, cold, and the wind howled as it blew across the deck. Jericho looked to the sky and stared at the stars. He kept his feet planted on the floor because his six-foot-seven-inch height and two-hundred-and-sixty-pound frame made the crate less sturdy. He tugged on his black and green camouflage jacket and ran his fingers through his short blond hair. Looking across the boat with his blue eyes, he let out a chuckle. The person sitting on another crate shivered in the cold air. That person was his brother and best friend, Tom Padilla. He was about six feet tall, with slicked-back black hair that reached his shoulders. He was a lighter shade Latino man, and his accent resurfaced when he was flustered. Even with his all-black clothes from head to toe, he was still cold. He constantly looked over at Jericho with an angry expression on his face.

"Come on, Tom." Jericho finally broke the silence. "This is our job."

"No, Jericho." Tom snapped back. "This is *your* job. I'm only here because you can't seem to find an assistant. And I wonder why. Psycho."

"Whoa! There's no need to get personal. Besides, I'm not the one who dropped the word Father from my name. What happened, Priest? Did you lose your faith?"

"Whatever, Caine." Tom waved his hand. "What happened out here anyway?"

"Vampire sirens are a special breed of vampires – all female." Jericho gazed out into the darkness. "Like all sirens, they use their melodious songs to lure sailors to the Reefs. They've been feeding on them for decades. I followed a tip, and as you know, I came here with my assistant Cameron. The sirens needed a supernatural as their king to help repopulate their species. Who else was a better choice than the slayer? Of course, I refused, and Cameron was murdered. I promised them I'd return one day for some payback. So, here we are."

Tom wiped his brow. "Yes. I remember when you told me

about poor Cameron. He was a good man, and by far, your best assistant."

Jericho turned back to Tom. "I agree. And now, I'm out here with a faithless priest."

Tom pointed at Jericho, who'd tried but couldn't keep in his laughter. "Hey. Don't start with that crap again. You know I never considered myself to be a priest anyway. Others did. Plus, your half-demon friend left me with no other choice but to leave the church. I couldn't put those people in danger anymore."

"I still stay; you guys are wrong about Hangy." Jericho crossed his legs at the ankles and fiddled with the scar over his left eye. "You'll see. There's a good explanation for what happened."

Tom clapped once. "Wake up, Caine. He killed BA. And we haven't seen or heard from him in over two weeks. He's probably plotting to kill us."

Jericho sighed. "Great. Here we go again."

"What? Of course, you think I'm wrong. But we need to be careful, big guy. He *does* have the Power Ring. Besides, you know something is off as well. You only rub that scar over your eye when you're confused. Then there's the issue of our backup. The wizard is off playing house. And…and Susie is still sidelined."

"Look, man." Jericho walked over and placed his hand on Tom's shoulder. "You know how much I like her. But she'll pull through. She's the toughest woman I've ever met. A little annoying, though."

They both laughed. Tom then leaned back against the boat

railing and crossed his legs. He looked down at his duffle bag, which sat next to his feet and sighed. He then stared up at Jericho, who noticed and frowned.

"What are you looking at, weirdo?" Jericho asked.

"I've been keeping something from you," Tom began. "And until I actually started believing this Death Brother's crap, I was going to keep it to myself."

Jericho twisted his lips. "Crap?"

"You know what I mean." Tom picked up his duffle bag. "You need to see this."

Tom unzipped the bag and pulled out what appeared to be a box, wrapped in a dirty rag. He pulled off the cloth and placed the object on his lap.

"Is that the book?" Jericho asked.

"Yes," Tom replied. "The Book of the Dead. I need to show you something, and it couldn't wait until we got back to New York."

"I hope it's as important as you think, Thomas. I thought we agreed to bring it out only in cases of emergency."

"It's important to us both, big guy. Trust me."

Tom opened the enormous black leather cased book and flipped the pages until he was almost at the end of the book. He handed the open book to Jericho.

"These final pages are about us...the Death Brothers," Tom said.

"Really? And you're just now showing me?"

Jericho took the book and walked back across the deck of the boat. He sat on the crate he'd been sitting on. The writing started with the story of Stephen and Patrick Dupree, the original Death Brothers.

"I know all this crap." Jericho glared at Tom. "I don't need a history lesson."

"Skip the first few pages, moron. Then you'll get to the good stuff."

Jericho continued to read. He glossed over how they were allowed to cheat death and bring each other back from the dead. He'd seen that act, twice. But his eyes opened wider when he got to the next two parts, which stated. *The brothers have a direct connection to angels. They also have a telepathic connection with each other.*

"Telepathy?" Jericho shot another glance at Tom. "Wow!"

Tom nodded. "I've been trying to use it ever since I read it. But I think your skull is too thick for it to work."

Jericho let out a sarcastic laugh. "Very funny. Not! You wanna give it a shot right now, I'm assuming."

"No. I just showed you the book because I wanted you to attempt to read at an adult level."

"I see you're on a roll tonight, Priest. But don't quit your day job. Now, come on. Let's try it."

Jericho and Tom straightened on their crates, and they stared into each other's eyes. They strained. The veins in their foreheads pultruded and pulsated. A slight headache set in and mucus drizzled from their noses

"Did you get that?" Jericho finally broke the silence.

"Get what?"

Jericho smiled. "I called you a hopeless virgin."

"You know I'm not a virgin, Caine," Tom dropped his head as his nose started to bleed...*jackass.*

"You don't have to get snippy, Tom. I don't call you names."

"You just *did!* But wait." Tom stood. "You heard that?"

"You calling me a jackass? Yes. What the hell for?"

"I didn't say that." Tom cocked his head to the side. "I *thought* it."

"Are you saying it worked?"

"I think so, big guy." Tom walked over and patted Jericho on the arm. "Let's try it again."

Jericho turned his head. "Hold up."

"What is it?"

Jericho stared out at the water. "I can see the lights from warning buoys. We're getting close." Jericho stood to face Tom. "We'll have to finish this later. Arm yourself."

Tom wrapped the Book of the Dead in the dingy cloth and put it back in his duffle bag. He fished around in the bag and pulled out a small glass vial of holy water.

Jericho smacked a wooden stake up against Tom's chest. "I'm not saying the holy water won't work. But I know this will."

Jericho reached down and picked up his own bag. He pulled out the Sword of Caine. He strapped on the brown sheath to his

10

back and slid the sword in it. He then began to place wooden stakes in a holster around his waist. He threw the straps of his bag over his shoulder. They were ready.

The tugboat stopped just before the beach. Jericho and Tom jump out their respective sides into the water that reached their knees. The swished as they walked to the sandy shore. It was dark, but they both noticed flies and a familiar smell…the smell of rotting flesh. They continued to walk, looking in all directions until Tom stumbled over a mound of sand. He fell onto his hands and knees and pushed himself back to his feet.

"Jeez, Priest," Jericho said, almost laughing. "Left, right, left, right. I'm sure you learned how to walk when you're were still a baby."

"Shut up, Jericho!" Tom looked down. "But I think we've found the source of the smell."

Jericho walked over to Tom and looked down as well. An arm stuck up out of the sand in what appeared to be a grave. Jericho reached in his duffle bag and pulled out an orange flare gun. He shot it in the air and watched as it illuminated the beach.

"My, God," Jericho said as he looked around. "There gotta be at least ten of these graves out here."

"Of what?"

"Could be victims, but I don't ever remember seeing these graves when I was here before."

Tom pointed further down the beach. "I think all of those torches headed this way are about to give us an answer."

Jericho unsheathed the Sword of Caine. "Be ready. We are not on friendly ground."

"Gotcha."

Downtown New York

A faint cloud of pink smoke hovered over one of the tallest buildings in the city. Thunder and lightning rang out throughout the sky, while rain drizzled down as well. Four large, round, gray metal conductors sat on the four corners of the rooftop. Thick wiring led from the conductors and met in the center of the roof. They were attached to a large wooden slab where a body lay covered under a white sheet. Doctor Noah Ranken, a short man with white slicked-back hair and glasses, ambled over to the table. He wore a white jacket, black slacks, and white tennis shoes. He placed his hands behind his back and turned toward the entrance to the rooftop.

"Must you always take so long, Grundy?" He asked. "We don't have all day. Nothing is better than natural power."

Grundy, a tall slider man with two large quarter-sized warts on each of his cheeks and a disfigured forehead, pushed a metal table over to the wooden slab. Most of Grundy's hair was gone. Oddly, a few long strings of gray hair were scattered over his large head. He also wore a long white jacket, and blue latex gloves covered his always shaky hands. He turned to the side and spit out a yellow substance. Most of his teeth were gone, only two front top teeth and his front bottom teeth remained. His brown eyes bulged as he hurriedly shuffled to stretch out the long jumper cables from the shelf underneath the table.

"Unfold the cables, Grundy," Dr. Ranken said. "Don't connect them. That is, not unless you want to fry too."

Grundy dropped the cables to the ground. "Yes, sir, Dr. Ranken."

"I didn't say, 'drop them to the ground either'!" Dr. Rankin picked up the cables and placed them gently across the covered body. "My God. How have I managed to achieve all this with your bumbling help?"

"I don't know, Dr. Ranken." Grundy walked back over toward the door and waited by a power lever on the wall, which were connected to the cables. "But, I appreciate your patience with me."

"Shut up, Grundy."

Dr. Ranken pulled off the bottom of the white sheet, exposing black boots with a small silver picks sticking out of each side. He attached two cables to each. He unraveled two more wires and pulled them toward the other end of the table. He rested them on the body and pulled back the sheet to expose the head of the body: it was a young man with gills on each side of his neck. He had long blonde hair. Two metal picks protruded from the sides of his neck, below the gills—Dr. Ranken attached the cables to each side.

"Pull the lever, Grundy," Dr. Ranken said. "It's time."

"Yes, sir, Doc." Grundy pulled the lever down.

Blue electric currents lit up the silver beacons.

"The beacons should attract any lightning." Dr. Ranken turned around in a circle and pointed at the beacons. "This will be my greatest achievement."

Lightning struck one of the beacons—an electric current shot into the body of the man on the table. The body lurched. That was it. Dr. Ranken looked into the man's face.

"Come on, dammit," He said. "Live."

With every lightning strike, Dr. Ranken's excitement faded. He dropped his head and placed his hands on his hips. He reached to the side, pulled the cart over, and sat on it. He simply stared at his most ambitious creation to date and shook his head.

The Gulf of Mexico

Jericho's eyes squinted as he tried to see who carried the torches that approached. He heard a piercing sound in the air and finally dove to the ground.

"Look out, Priest," Jericho yelled as he jumped back to his feet after an arrow landed to the side of his body. "Doesn't appear that they're in a talkative mood."

Tom began looking around. "How are we supposed to see arrows in the dark?"

"Hold on," Jericho said as he raised his sword in the air.

The Sword of Caine began to glow and brightened the beach. About twenty vampire sirens surrounded Jericho and Tom. Two sirens held bow and arrows and prepared to fire. The others held torches and hissed as their fangs pultruded from their mouths.

"Screw this waiting crap," Tom said as he drew back the wooden stake.

Tom launched the stake into one of the siren's chest, who held a bow. She looked down at the stake and tried to pull it out. It was too late. Her eyes bulged as she stared back up at Tom and then burst into ashes. Another siren charged at Jericho. He spun around and chopped off her head. Before her headless body hit the ground, it burst into fiery ashes. Tom and Jericho then stood back to back and waited for the rest of the sirens to attack.

"Stop!" A voice yelled out in the distance.

The sirens stood aside to open a space between them, Jericho and Tom. A taller red-headed siren walked up to the opening.

"We've been expecting you, but I didn't think it would be so soon, Slayer," She said. "I was hoping we had a little more time."

Jericho straightened from his fight stance. "Well. Well. Well. If it is Princess Vivian. I gave you guys my word that I'd be back for the rest of you. And I always try to keep my word."

"We're of no threat to you, Slayer," Vivian said. "We only defend ourselves when necessary."

Jericho pointed his sword at her. "I owe it to Cameron, my former assistant, who you and your sisters killed."

"Haven't you all done enough to us?" She spread out her hands. "Look at our numbers. Didn't your doctor take enough from us?"

"My doctor?" Jericho glanced at Tom. "What, doctor?"

"Yes, what, doctor?" Tom asked.

"He came here and took our brother." She said.

Jericho lowered his sword as the siren continued to walk toward him. He thought back to when he and his assistant Cameron were there before. Their queen wanted to marry Jericho to help repopulate their coven. He remembered it was impossible to produce a male siren.

Jericho burst into laughter. "Are you trying to get us to pity you by telling us some silly sob story, which happens to be a lie? There are no male sirens. There can't be."

Jericho raised his sword again and took a step toward her.

"Wait!" Vivian held up her hand. "You know our story, Slayer, and how we came to exist. Our mother, Queen Retta, slept with a male mermaid, Thaddeus, and produced our unique race. What we didn't know is that Queen Retta did bare Thaddeus a son. Thaddeus took the child to be raised with the mermaids. His name was Thaden, and he returned to us as an adult-only recently. He wanted to get to know his sisters. However, a doctor from the States appeared in the middle of the day with the sun as his ally. He knew what we were, and he wanted only one thing – our brother Thaden. We couldn't fight back as they launched garlic grenades and holy water into our catacombs." She dropped her head. "We lost many of our sisters. He promised he'd stop the bombardment if Thaden surrendered. I pleaded with Thaden to wait until the sun had set so we could properly defend ourselves, but he didn't want anyone else to die. So, he surrendered. I yelled out, 'why are you doing this?' He said, 'ask my friend Jericho Caine.' I then watched helplessly as they boarded a boat and set sail."

Jericho lowered his weapon again and stepped backward to whisper to Tom. "I think she's telling the truth, buddy. What's your take on it?"

Tom leaned forward to Jericho's ear. "I do too. What now?"

Jericho sighed and looked around at the sirens. They were still on guard but didn't appear as though they wanted a fight. He studied their faces. He noticed something that he didn't think he'd ever see in creatures of the night…sorrow. He believed Vivian. *Their brother Thaden was abducted by someone claiming to know me. But who? And why?*

"And you didn't get a name?" Jericho turned back to Vivian. "Anything?"

"No." She replied. "I did see the name on the side of the barge. It said, 'It's Alive.' The fact that he mentioned your name let me know that you'd be coming soon."

"Well, did you at least get a decent look at him?" Tom asked

"He was a short white man with white hair and glasses," Vivian said. "That's all I saw even with my vampire's eyes."

Jericho turned to the side and nodded. "Ok. I believe you. But I still can't let Cameron's death go unpunished."

Jericho leaped into the air and launched at Vivian. He came down with his sword out front and rammed it into her chest. He yanked his sword away and watched Vivian stagger backward. She clutched her chest. She moved her head around to stare at her sisters.

"Take no vengeance." Vivian fell to her knees. "We had a debt to pay."

Vivian slowly began to turn to ashes, which blew away in the wind. Jericho stepped backward until he was again back to back with Tom. They were ready for an attack. However, the sirens just hissed and slowly backed away. They disappeared into the night.

"You wanna go after them?" Tom asked, "I mean, we did come here to dust them all."

"No." Jericho continued to stare out into the darkness. "Her death will do…for now."

"What now then?"

"We go home. Something strange is in motion, and I fear we may be too late to stop it."

New York

Finally, as if it were alive, a portion of the smoky pink haze that hovered over the building began to descend. Dr. Ranken stood and took a step backward. He turned to Grundy with a confused expression and nodded toward the body on the table. Grundy hunched.

"Of course, Grundy," Dr. Ranken said. "You don't seem to know anything right now."

Dr. Ranken turned back to the body. Suddenly, a small portion of the pink smoke streamed into the body's nose.

Dr. Ranken quickly turned back to Grundy again. "This is it. Throw the switch, Grundy!"

Grundy pulled the lever again. The metal conductors began to vibrate, and a bolt of lightning shot down and struck the beacons. The body started to hemorrhage and glow bright pink as electricity poured into him. Dr. Ranken smiled. He knew what was happening was not what he envisioned, but it was happening none-the-less.

The body's eyes opened. They were black. The creature looked from side to side as the rain poured on his face. He turned and glared at Grundy and then Dr. Ranken. He tried to sit up, but his arms and legs were still strapped to the wooden table.

"Release me," he said as he stared at Dr. Ranken.

"Release yourself." Dr. Ranken smiled and interlocked his hands behind his back. "You are more powerful than you know."

Dr. Ranken grabbed the white sheet that still covered the body and pulled it off. The creature looked down and saw horizontal stitches that stretched from his neck down to the white shorts that covered his groin area.

"Wh-what have you done to me?" He asked.

Dr. Ranken walked over and placed his hand on the man's forehead. "I have made you into the most dangerous creature on earth."

"But how?" The man asked.

"Concentrate, my son." Dr. Ranken looked down at the man's body. "Feel your power, and then show it."

The man closed his eyes and then opened them quickly. They glowed red. He balled his fist. Hair grew the left half of his body until it was completely covered with black fur. His forehead crumpled as he stared back at Dr. Ranken.

"What is this?" He asked.

"You are the only male vampire siren." Dr. Ranken rubbed his hands together. "Your name is Thaden. I have replaced half of your body with a werewolf. The werewolf side has your new heart, so a stake won't kill you. Your werewolf attributes should make you immune to the sun. You will still have all the abilities that come from being a vampire siren and a werewolf. You are now perfect, my son."

Thaden raised his arms, snapping the leather restraints around his wrists. He spun around to the sides and snapped them on his ankles. He sat up and moved his head from side to side. A cracking noise sounded off as he stood in a puddle of water beneath him. He was about seven feet tall and towered over Dr. Ranken.

"Why me?" Thaden asked.

"For the oldest reason in the book," Dr. Ranken said. "Revenge."

"Revenge? Against whom?"

"The so-called Death Brothers." Dr. Ranken slowly approached and stared up into Thaden's red eyes. "You will find that we have a lot in common. The so-called Death Brothers is that commonality. They are responsible for the death of your sister, the great Queen Jetta. They are also responsible for the death and ruination of my family's name: I am the descendent of Ernest Frankenstein. His brother, Victor Frankenstein, was the genius who came up with cellular regeneration. In the mid-eighteen hundredths, my family had finally put to rest the tragedy of the Frankenstein Monster. My father found Victor's notes and dabbled with a few of his experiments. The first incarnation of the Death Brothers stormed Ernest's private estate and killed him. They torched anything related to him and Victor's work."

"So, I'm your Frankenstein monster?" Thaden's vampire teeth began to pultrude from his mouth. "I am nobody's monster."

Dr. Ranken held up his hands. "No. No, my son. You are much more than that. And if you give me the time, I will show you how much more."

Part II

Sariel

Six Months Ago

The lamp on the brown wooden nightstand clicked on. The man sleeping in the bed turned over but didn't awaken. Finally, the lamp was smashed over his head. He quickly sat up and brushed the broken pieces to the floor. He reached over to the nightstand and felt around for his glasses. He put them on and stared around the darkened room. The moonlight provided some light, but only a large shadow loomed in the far corner of the room. The man squinted and tried to focus on the shadow.

"Wh-who's there?" He asked. "I have a weapon."

"Dr. Noah Ranken." A woman's voice spoke out. "We both know you don't have a weapon. Now, calm yourself, and let's talk."

"Who are you?" Dr. Ranken asked as he leaned forward to try and get a better look at the stranger in his room. "I don't have any money."

"I know, doctor," the stranger said. "You've almost gone broke while working on your little pet project. And that's what I'm here to talk to you about."

"Well, you're obviously a woman. That much is for sure," Dr. Ranken said. "But what do you want from me and my work."

"I want to help you." The woman straightened and walked toward the bed. "You can help me get what I want. And I, in turn, can help you get what you want."

"And how do *you* know what I want?"

"Because my name is Sariel." She stepped into the moonlight, revealing her long blond hair, white gown, and wings. "And I am an angel. I have the gift of seeing where an object has been and where it is going."

"So, you can see the future?"

"Of an object, not a person." Sariel surveyed the room, walked over to the dresser, and picked up the loose change. "For instance, I can see that you will purchase a bottle of water from the local convenience store with this later."

"And what If I don't, simply because you've just told this to me."

"Then the object's future will change. But for now, that is the future of this currency."

Dr. Ranken swung his feet out to the floor and placed them in his slippers. He stared at the money as Sariel put it back on the dresser and stared into her face. Her eyes were black, so he couldn't peer into them. He stood and slowly walked toward her.

"So, what do you want from me, angel?" He asked.

I want to help you use your project to help me. And by doing so, you will get at least half of what you want."

"Half?"

"Simply put, I want the slayer, doctor. But not to kill. However, you can do whatever you want with the priest."

"No!" Dr. Ranken pounded his fist into his other hand. "My vengeance ends with both of their lives extinguished. Now, what's it to you if we kill the slayer too?"

"I have my reasons. Besides, you won't even be able to kill the priest without my help. Your creation won't last five seconds."

Dr. Ranken turned his back to Sariel and stroked his chin. "How do you know this?"

"Your creation will live. But I can make it better. I can make it more powerful."

There was a long silence until Dr. Ranken held out his hand toward the door. "Hmm. Follow me."

Dr. Ranken led Sariel out of the bedroom to the elevators. He pushed the button marked "Basement" and waited in silence for the elevator to go down sixty stories to the basement level. Dr. Ranken pulled out a skeleton key from his robe pocket, and they walked down a long hallway leading to a massive metal door. He unlocked it and hesitated.

"Don't worry, doc," Sariel said as she pushed past Dr. Ranken. "I'm not here to steal your work. I'm here to help."

They entered the room, and Dr. Ranken flipped the light switch on the wall. Bright lights embedded in the ceiling lit up what turned out to be a lab. A computer sat on a large desk against one wall. Bookshelves with books and potions lined the other walls. In the center of the lab was a large gurney with a covered body on top.

Sariel walked over and pulled the white sheet off the body. "Yes. The male vampire siren."

She touched its head and looked to the ceiling. Her eyes glowed white, and a smile consumed her face. She glanced at Dr. Ranken and nodded.

"I like this," she said. "The sirens could not have been happy when you took him."

"They weren't. But how are you gonna make it better? 'More powerful?'"

"By adding something that simple electricity can't bring to life."

"What's that?"

"A werewolf. I just happen to know the location of a corpse."

A werewolf?" Dr. Ranken quickly walked up to Sariel and stared up into her nearly six-nine face. "What do you mean exactly?"

"Exactly what you think I mean. I want you to split this body right down the middle. Keep the face, though. He's cute. The other half will be a werewolf without the head."

"Is that possible?" Dr. Ranken's forehead crumpled. "That will require more skills than I possess."

"Leave that to me. But you'll know it when you see it." She turned and saw a photo on the wall of Dr. Ranken and Dr. Grundy. "You will need Dr. Grundy too. Believe it or not, Doc, he's more intelligent than even you. The only reason I'm here with you, and not him, is because of your dedication to destroying the Death Brothers. Your work can be duplicated by anyone, but the difference is, you have faith in yours. We will, however, literally, need Grundy's brain."

"Meaning?"

"I'll let you know that part when the time is right." She turned and walked toward the door. "But for now, continue your work. When you hear from me again, I will have everything you need to begin the final phase."

Harvey, Illinois

The Hangman, like many nights, sat on the roof of his old house in the center of Delaware Street. He sat with his legs hanging off the edge of the roof. He looked both ways down the empty street. Yellow police barricades were posted on at the end of the road and on the sidewalks. No one had lived on the street since he terrorized it when he first returned to Earth as the Hangman.

He sighed as he stared up at the full moon. *I finally have my wish. I'm the most powerful being on the planet, and I'm bored to death—none of its worth it without my Dorothy and Kente Jr.* The Hangman remembered the last day he saw his wife and son when he was Kente Cromwell Sr. It was the morning he'd died. Dorothy

26

made homemade waffles with bacon and eggs. They sat around the breakfast table and talked about him retiring soon and leaving Cromwell Construction in the hands of Dorothy's brother, Joseph.

However, Kente Sr. didn't make it home that night as he was murdered by the jealous men on Delaware Street. Thus, bringing about the carnage from the reborn Hangman. Suddenly, he turned his head quickly from side to side and began to sniff the air.

"I don't' like people spying on me," he said. "Especially angels."

Sariel appeared standing next to the Hangman. She sat next to him with her legs folded.

"Easy, tough guy." She put up her hand. "I'm not here to fight. Although, after what you did to BA, there are a ton of angels wanting to come here and do just that."

"So why are you here? And don't say it's to warn me."

"I'm here to offer you a deal in exchange for a favor of sorts."

"What's my benefit of the deal, first?"

"I will help you get your family back, and keep Caine and Padilla occupied while you're doing it."

"You can do this?"

"It's what I do. I make deals all the time. I will be calling in some major favors to do it, but it can be done."

"*For me?*"

"No one has to know it's for you."

"And what do you want in return?"

"The Life Bringer spell has fallen into my hands. But you are the only being on earth, along with that ring of yours, who can use it."

"What will I be bringing back to life?"

"Almost any supernatural creatures that the spell comes into contact with. And I have chosen New York for this operation."

"Hmm." The Hangman folded his arms. "That is definitely the place to occupy Caine's and Padilla's attention. But now, what's in it for you?"

"Chaos and anarchy." She stood and put her hands on her hips. "It will be worth my fall from grace when my involvement is revealed."

The Hangman laughed. "Wow, you angels must really hate humans. There is always one of you lurking about trying to destroy humanity."

"More than you know, my friend."

"We're not friends…angel. Because let me be clear." The Hangman stood and was face to face with Sariel. "If this is some kind of trick, or I'm not reunited with my family, what I did to BA will seem like mercy when I'm finished with you."

"Well, then we'd better not screw this up, I'm guessing."

"Indeed."

One Week Ago

Dr. Grundy walked over and stood behind Dr. Ranken, who was sitting at his computer desk.

"I've completed the Encephalon Transference Modulation

helmets." Dr. Grundy clapped his hands together. "But I still don't know why we need it. There's no one around to test it on."

"I thought you were a genius, Grundy," Dr. Ranken stopped typing. "Is this what you have to offer to this project…questions?"

"I don't get it, Noah." Dr. Grundy tilted his head to the side. "For a week now, you've been making snide remarks about my intelligence. And frankly, some of it has been flat-out rude. I was there when no one wanted to work with you because they said you were a mad man. *Me*. No one else."

"I'm sorry, Moses." Dr. Ranken sighed. "But this project is starting to wear on me, especially with the modifications that we've made."

"And that's another thing. Why did we make those modifications? Everything was seemingly on schedule for next week."

"Well, I-I – "

Dr. Grundy fell forward onto Dr. Ranken's back and then to the floor. Dr. Ranken jumped to his feet and spun around to see Sariel holding a steel pipe.

"What in the hell are you doing, she-angel?" Dr. Ranken he fell backward against a filing cabinet. "This isn't what we discussed."

"It is exactly that, Doc." Sariel peered down at Dr. Grundy. "It's time."

"Time for what?"

"What do you think? We are going to transfer Dr. Grundy's

intelligence into your creation. It's a shame that never dawned on him while he was building it."

"You're mad." Dr. Ranken stared into Sariel's cold black eyes. "I never agreed to this."

"But you did, Noah," she said. "Just as you'll agree with what comes next. Now, drag his body over to the gurney, and let's begin. I had to pull a lot of strings to get to this moment."

"My God," Dr. Ranken grabbed his chest. "You actually want to transfer Grundy's intellect to my creation?"

"No disrespect to you. But I'm doing the thinking for both of us, Dr. Ranken." She folded her arms. "You may not always be around. Extra measures are warranted."

Dr. Ranken grabbed Grundy's ankles and dragged the doctor over to the wooden gurney. He used a white dry-towel to wipe off the blood on the back of Grundy's head. He grabbed Grundy's project off the table, the ETM, which consisted of two metal helmets. A thick wire tube connected the helmets. Dr. Ranken placed a helmet on Thaden's head and the other on Grundy's head. He pushed a red button on the back of Grundy's helmet. A humming sound ensued as both bodies began to shake.

Sariel smiled. "I believe that sound means it's working."

"But did we really have sacrifice, Grundy?"

"Yes. And don't play innocent with me, Doc. You became spiteful towards him as soon as I told you he was more intelligent than you."

"That's why you told me that, isn't it?" Dr. Ranken frowned.

"You may be an angel, but you have all the traits of a scorned human woman."

"I'll take that as a compliment. Now, make Mr. Grundy comfortable. At least you'll have free labor if you play this the right way. I must go and make sure the other pieces of the chessboard are where they need to be. Plus, thanks to me, you will have a supernatural army to back you up. Just be a little more patient."

Three Days Ago

Jericho awoke. It was about eight o'clock in the morning. He yawned and stretched while still lying flat on his back. He looked around and remembered where he'd fallen asleep. It was in Tom's spare bedroom. Surprisingly, the twin bed was large enough to hold the enormous vampire slayer's body. However, his feet hung over the edge, and part of his arm hung out as well. He swung his legs to the floor and looked over in the far corner. As usual, when he awoke, he located his black duffle bag, which housed The Sword of Caine.

He put on his socks and stood. He smelled the aroma of bacon in the air. *Ah, the priest is awake as well…and cooking. Hope he made a lot because I'm starving.* Jericho took a step toward the closed door and stopped as he looked down and saw a red bandana on the floor.

"What the hell?" Jericho bent down and picked it up. "This is Cameron's. But how did it end up here?"

Jericho looked at the window. It was closed and still locked.

He walked over to it and looked out. *Even if the window were unlocked, someone would have had to climbed up five stories to put the bandana in the room.* Jericho scratched his head and walked out of the room. He went down a short blue hallway toward the kitchen. He let out a chuckle as he saw Tom, dressed in his usual black shirt and pants, but with a white apron tied around his waist.

"I hope you're not laughing at me," Tom said. "If so, it looks like I'll be the only one eating breakfast today."

"Calm down, man." Jericho sat at the small table in the kitchen. "Why do you always think I'm laughing at you?"

Tom twisted his lips. "Because you always are. You're a big kid, Jericho."

"Whatever, Priest." Jericho pulled out the bandana. "Do you know how this got in my room? I found it on the floor."

Tom studied the bandana. "Nope. No clue. But that belonged to Cameron, right? I hated seeing that thing wrapped around his head."

"Yes, it was Cameron's." Jericho stuffed the bandana back in his pocket. "But if you didn't put it there, how did it get there?"

"You probably got drunk and left it, Caine."

"No, I didn't. Besides, you know I can't get drunk with my healing ability. Maybe it's Cameron trying to get me to keep my word."

"No way!" Tom pulled off the apron and threw it on the table. "We're trying to get back to a sense of normalcy, big guy. Now's not the time to go off on some foolhardy mission."

"Listen." Jericho pounded his fist on the table. "I gave Cameron and those sirens my word that I would avenge his death. This has to be a sign. Now, are you with me, Priest?"

Tom sat in the other chair and stared into Jericho's face. "Under one condition."

"Name it."

"You stop calling me Priest."

"Done."

"That was a little too quick and easy." Tom picked up a knife and fork lying next to his plate. "Now, let's eat and then figure this out. I don't wanna starve before we go give the vampire sirens a chance to kill us."

Harvey, Illinois

The Hangman sat in what used to be his favorite leather recliner chair. He stared into the empty fireplace. The living room was still furnished, but dust covered most of the furniture. He was startled by a knock at the front door. *Who is crazy enough to come here? Nobody comes here.*

The Hangman stood and walked to the front door. The Power Ring, which covered three of his fingers, glowed pink. He looked out the peephole and saw a blinding white light. *I should have known.*

He opened the door. "Why are you knocking? Couldn't you just have appeared inside the house?"

"I don't like showing off." Sariel smiled and slowly walked

past the Hangman. "Besides, I didn't want to surprise you, and you get trigger-happy with that ring."

"Fair enough. What do you have for me?"

"Your family will be in Purgatory at a specific time for just one hour." Sariel interlocked her hands behind her back and paced the living room. "That is your window, and it will be your one and only chance to retrieve them. That was the best I could do."

"I will be there." The Hangman sat back down in his chair. "Will there be any opposition?"

"The angel that owes me will have them there. Guaranteed." She sighed. "But the guardian of Purgatory is not in on this. So, it is in your best interest to be stealthy and quick."

"Ok. Those terms are agreeable. I'll assume you'll let me know when I can expect to do this?"

"I will."

"Ok. Did you bring the spell?"

Sariel pulled a worn piece of paper from her pocket. "Here it is. But you'll only get one shot at this. Once the spell is used, you can't use it again. And it can only be used with the Power Ring."

"Hmm." The Hangman's fiery red eyes glowed. "But I still want to know, what's in this for you, angel? I'm not buying that 'chaos and anarchy' bit."

"Let's just say that I have business with the Death Brothers. This will ensure that my plan works out…one way or the other."

The Hangman laughed. "Looks like Caine and Padilla have pissed off more than just the underworld."

"Well, the spell only covers a space as big as a city. So, make sure you're in New York in three days to complete it."

"Sure thing."

Part III

Home, Sweet Home?

New York, Present Day

Jericho stood back and waited for Tom to take out his keys. "Did you happen to notice the pinkish sky?"

"I did," Tom replied. "Something tells me we'll find out what that's all about real soon."

Jericho and Tom walked into Tom's apartment. Jericho collapsed on the black leather couch and placed a cold bottle of beer against his temple. Tom sank into the adjacent and matching recliner. They both let out a deep sigh. Tom reached out and grabbed the remote control for the thirty-two-inch TV facing them on the TV stand. He cut on the TV and sank back into the chair.

"I see the demon-hunting business doesn't pay that well." Jericho chuckled. "Can you even see when words appear on that little screen? How does it even have a remote control?"

Tom looked over a Jericho and smiled. "You know, everyone

can't just take what they want when they want it, big guy. Some of us like to earn what we have. It's what heroes do."

"Earn?" Jericho erupted in fake laughter. "Dude. The church gave that to you…as a donation. That's kinda like charity."

"Shouldn't you be trying to figure out why someone, who knows you, is kidnapping vampire sirens? It's probably someone trying to kill you. Although I can definitely see why."

"Jesus, Tom!" Jericho sat up and placed the beer on the table. "Do you keep me around because you're lonely? Because all I hear out of you is criticisms of my methods."

Tom picked up Jericho's beer, laughed, and took a sip. "Methods? Is that what you call them now? I thought it was, 'I'm Jericho Caine, the big badass vampire slayer. I'm here to go all Willy-Nilly and destroy everything I touch'. Methods…yeah, right."

"You're just jealous because I've dusted twice as many vampires than demons that you could ever hunt."

Tom stood. "Are you insane? Demons are way tougher than vampires."

"Oh yeah? Then why is there someone collecting vampire sirens and not demons?"

"That was my original point, moron. Jeez!"

There was a long silence. Jericho lay back down. *Dammit! Tom is right. I guess there's no rest for the weary.* Jericho thought back to his time at the Reefs and his run-in with the vampire angel Dakota. He couldn't remember any other humans involved, other than his assistant Cameron. Nothing could explain why a human would abduct the only male vampire siren. *Who else would know about the phenomenon of a male vampire siren? It's kinda like a werewolf. They are so rare that the angels took the body of the only one I killed. I wonder if there's a connection.*

"Hey, Priest?" Jericho sat up again.

"Stop calling me that. Does your word mean anything to you?"

"Sorry. Tom, then. This may be nothing, but I need you to do me a favor."

"Spit it out."

"I need you to use that *'connection to the angels'* crap and call on your winged friend, Arellos."

"Oh. So, it's *crap* when you don't like something. But it's our *destiny* when you want to try something new? Why?" Tom spread out his arms. "After BA fell in battle, they aren't too happy with either of us right now."

"I need an answer to a question that's starting to bother me."

"And the angels have the answer?"

"Yes. They should."

Downtown New York

Dr. Ranken entered the vast dining area in his loft. It had a twenty-foot table in the center that was covered by a white cloth. Only one chair sat at each end of the table. An antique grandfather clock stood in the corner, and ancient weaponry was scattered along the walls throughout the room.

"I'm ready," Dr. Ranken said as he sat and placed and napkin in his lap.

The swinging door behind the doctor opened, and Grundy, wearing a black suit, entered the room. He pushed a tray with a silver lid covering a platter. He pulled up the lid, and steam rose from roasted lamb, mashed potatoes, and boiled carrots.

"I hope you enjoy it, Doc." Grundy walked back toward the door.

"Is our new friend cleaned up?"

"Yes, sir. He is."

"Well, send him in."

Dr. Ranken picked up a steak knife and fork; he cut a small piece of the lamb, and blood dribbled out. He shook his head and turned the plate until the mashed potatoes were in front of him. He began eating.

"Dammit. I told Grundy I don't like my meat that rare." He sprinkled salt and pepper on the meal. "But then again, he does have the intellect of a fruit-fly right now."

"You don't want it?" A deep voice from behind said. "I'll take it. The canine side of me hungers."

Dr. Ranken stood and turned around. "Thaden, my son. Come. Sit and eat. Grundy!"

Grundy entered the room, pushing another platter with a larger portion of lamb. It was barely cooked. Dr. Ranken reached down and pulled a tattered brown book from the satchel on the floor beside him. He placed it on the table and watched as Thaden grabbed the lamb with both hands and began to devour it. His vampire's teeth were replaced by his canine teeth. His left arm and hand were covered with black fur. He grunted, and saliva dripped from the side of his mouth as he continued to eat.

"Are you ready to learn more about why you exist, my son?" Dr. Ranken asked. "It is all right here in this book."

Thaden swallowed the last of the lamb and licked his lips. "Indeed, I am. But there's a new wrinkle in all this." He motioned for Grundy to come over. "We won't be needing this dim-witted idiot any longer."

Thaden reached up and grabbed Grundy by the throat. With a simple twist of his wrist, Thaden snapped Grundy's neck. The body went limp and collapsed to the floor. Thaden then looked over at Dr. Ranken, whose mouth hung open.

"He was the third wheel that we no longer need," Thaden said. "Now, tell me why you have brought me to life."

Dr. Ranken swallowed hard. "And how do I know this isn't the fate that awaits me one day?"

"Let's just hope you don't ever become useless, doctor." Thaden reached out and took the lamb from Dr. Ranken's plate. "I'm famished. Now, talk."

"Um, it's simple." Dr. Ranken picked up the book again. "The answers are in here. The Death Brothers are the vampire slayer, Jericho Caine, and the demon hunter, Father Thomas Padilla. They are the reincarnation of the famed Death Brothers, who were a vampire hunter and werewolf hunter. They represent the supernatural police here on earth. And with you, my vengeance will now be at hand."

"I will not kill them for you." Thaden licked his fingers. "But I will kill them because they stand in the way of me taking over this city…and then eventually, the world. If their deaths also get revenge for you, then so be it."

"Beware, though, Thaden."

"I prefer to be called Lord Thaden from now on."

"My apologies, *Lord Thaden*. But there may be a wrinkle. A female angel has made herself known. She is also part of the reason you are here. She wants to keep the vampire slayer alive and doesn't care what happens to the priest. She went so far as to promise us a supernatural army as well."

"Interesting." Thaden rubbed his chin. "If her services are no longer needed, I guess I'll get to kill an angel as well. Make no mistake: these Death Brothers must surely die. And I will destroy anyone that tries to stop me…angels included. By the way, have you noticed that the pink cloud is still hovering over the city?"

"I have."

"And?"

Dr. Ranken shrugged his shoulders. "And what? I don't know."

Thaden sighed and snatched the book out of Dr. Ranken's hand. He stood and walked out of the dining area. He headed for his private quarters. As he walked past the kitchen, he took another slab of lamb and began eating as he walked into his room. He sat on the bed and turned on the lamp sitting on the nearby nightstand. He laid back against the bed frame and raised his feet into the bed. He glared around the room and looked at the photos of the Ranken's family history. He figured he was in the right place for what he was about to read.

The Journal

July 5, 1888

It has been a year since my son Darren was born, and we've moved to the New World in America. I want to finish my work now. We had to leave Europe and start over. I've decided to keep the Frankenstein name, and hopefully, restore it to prominence. My brother Victor was a genius but labeled a madman after the monster he created became a psychotic murderer. He terrorized a small town and eventually killed Victor as well. Now, I've restored my brother's notes and plan to finish what he started.

July 13, 1888

There is a piece to the regenerative formula that I have missed or misinterpreted. I am stuck until I figure it out. I was also visited by two strange men today, claiming they were bible salesmen. They dressed in all grey and black leather. The one who spoke said his name was Stephen. They had scars on their faces and appeared to be in a not-so-friendly mood. I'm sure they weren't bible salesmen. They asked what my name was, and I told them it was Josiah

Ranken. I didn't want to give out my real name because I honestly didn't know what they were after. As they talked at the front door, the other man moved his head from side to side, trying to look inside the house.

"My final answer is no," I said, feeling uncomfortable with the other man's gaze. "I don't want to be rude, but I'm going to close the door now."

"Ok...*Mr. Ranken*, was it?" Stephen pulled out a small piece of paper. "This is where you can find us if you change your mind. Or, if you *need* our help."

I closed the door and watched as the two men walked back toward the dirt road and turned around to stare at the house. So, I went upstairs to check on Marie and the little Darren. They were fine, so I went back to the cellar and continued trying to decipher my brother's notes.

July 20, 1888

Yes! I have figured it out. The regeneration formula is complete, and I can begin testing it. Luckily, I have started working in the town coroner's office with a fresh supply of resources almost daily. The formula is as follows. I...

...and now I am fearful of the safety of my family. I have come to learn that Stephen and his brother Patrick are, in fact, known as the Death Brothers. They originated from Europe and are a remarkably young, considering I was told they've been in the States since the late seventeen hundredths. I didn't even know vampires and werewolves existed. They appear to be fixated with my work, and I'm wondering if I should pause.

The Present

"Wait a minute." Thaden sat up in the bed. "There are pages torn out. The regeneration formula, in particular, is gone."

Thaden got to his feet and looked out the window at the full moon. He balled his fists, raised them, and stared at them. Strange energy coursed through his body: he felt powerful. He bent down and grabbed the wooden leg of his bed, and pulled it off. He began to squeeze until the wooden leg exploded in his hands. His eyes popped open. *Must be the werewolf side of me reacting to the full moon. I think I'm going to like this.*

But Thaden wanted answers. He knew Dr. Ranken either had the torn pages or didn't know where they were. Either way, he knew he had to confront the doctor. Thaden walked down to Dr. Ranken's lab, where the doctor was mixing a formula.

"You didn't trust me with the formula?" Thaden asked as he entered the lab. "That's not very nice, considering we're partners."

Dr. Ranken frowned and tilted head to the side. "What are you talking about? What formula?"

"The one in the journal." Thaden held up the journal. "I thought we were as one in this."

Dr. Ranken took the journal and stared at the gaps in the pages. "I don't understand. It was here."

"Well, who could have taken it, Doctor?" Thaden asked.

"Who else would even know what it was, and have access to it?"

Dr. Ranken leaned his hands on the lab table and lowered his head while closing his eyes. The vein swelled in the middle of his forehead. He opened eyes with concern in his face.

"Grundy." Dr. Ranken shook his head. "He's the only one who could have done this."

"What do you think he was up to?" Thaden asked. "He no longer had the intellect to do anything with it. And now he's dead."

"No thanks to you." Dr. Ranken drummed his fingers on the lab desk. "Dammit. It's just as I feared. He started acting weird when the angel got involved. He probably took the pages before we did the brain transference."

"I see," Thaden said. "And I don't have his memories. Does that mean that the formula is lost?"

"I'm afraid so." Dr. Ranken sighed. "The formula might be lost forever. But that might not be a bad thing."

"No!" Thaden thundered. "I want that formula. I have plans."

"You have plans that you haven't shared with me?" Dr. Ranken frowned. "Who's being the bad partner now?"

Thaden smiled. "I was going to bring you in on the plans later, my good doctor. But let's just concentrate on finding the formula."

Dr. Ranken nodded. "Agreed."

"And to be safe, we should get some insurance for our supernatural crime fighters. My research tells me it's located in San Diego."

A devious smile appeared on Dr. Ranken's face, "I like the

way you think."

Jericho walked around Tom's apartment and wondered how his best friend's living conditions were almost the total opposite of his own. He enjoyed the company of women and liquor, even though he couldn't get drunk. He liked being social, enjoyed watching television, and listening to music. *This apartment is practically empty, except for the essential functions. Come on, Tom. This is sad.*

Jericho placed his duffle bag on the sofa and pulled out the Sword of Caine. He wanted to be ready, just in case. Because he knew Tom was right. After the Hangman killed BA, the angels would probably not be thrilled to hear from them either. Jericho sat with the sword across his lap and waited as Tom reentered the room.

"You sure about this, big guy?" Tom asked as he also gripped the brass knuckles tighter that were on each of his hands. "This might not go our way."

"I have a hunch, Tom. Do it."

Tom dropped to his knees in the center of the room and bowed his head. He pressed his hands together to pray.

"Arellos, guardian of the Nether Region, please come to me for aide. I need your guidance."

Jericho gripped the handle of his sword tightly and looked in around in all directions. He was prepared for anything. He didn't want to stand because he didn't' want to give the impression of a hostile situation. He listened as Tom repeated the prayer. Suddenly, the lightbulb in the lamp began to flicker, and the television turned off. When the light stopped flickering, a massive shadow appeared in the corner.

"Wow." Arellos' voice boomed throughout the living room. "You two have some nerve."

"Forgive us," Tom said. "I know we're not the most popular people in Heaven right now, but we have some questions."

"You mean the slayer has questions, right?" Arellos asked. "You're a better friend than he gives you credit for, Thomas."

"Are you here to help or make us feel worse than we already do?" Jericho asked as he stood. "Screw it. Don't help. We will figure this out no matter how long it takes. We're not going to grovel."

Arellos stepped into the light, revealing the seven-foot frame. He had long blond hair, black sunglasses, and wore a white trench coat.

"I can see why you and BA often clashed, Slayer." Arellos nodded at Jericho. "You can put the sword away. I will gladly answer your question. Besides, regardless of what has happened, you two still have an important part to play in things to come."

"And let me guess," Jericho lay the sword on the couch. "You're not going to tell us what that part is either? Or the things that are coming?"

"Nope."

"Just ask your question, Jericho." Tom cut in. "We didn't call on him to argue."

"Fine," Jericho said. "You remember when I got rid of that vampire angel for you guys, right? Angels swooped in after the fight and took the corpse of a werewolf. Where to?"

"I remember," Arellos replied. "But the tone in your voice makes it seem like we should be in your debt for doing your job. Besides, I seem to recall me leading a mission into the Sword of Caine to rescue and return your soul to your body not too long ago."

"Hold on. Hold on." Tom put up his hand. "Please, Arellos, don't give in to Caine's combative nature. It's what he does. We just need his question answered."

Arellos smiled. "Again, I can see why he needs you. But to answer your question, we took the corpse to purgatory. Strange that you ask, though."

"Why strange?" Tom asked.

"The corpse was just stolen a week ago." Arellos continued.

"Stolen?" Jericho glared at Tom and then back at Arellos. "Do you know by whom?"

"No, sadly." Arellos paced the floor with his hands behind his back. "But one thing's for sure. It could have only been an angel."

"Oh, there's a shocker." Jericho shook his head. "Another crooked angel. "No surprises there."

"Now, you hold on, Slayer." Arellos walked up and stood in front of Jericho. "Those are my brothers and sisters you're talking about. We're still the good guys."

Jericho smiled. "Or so you s – "

"You're right." Tom cut in. "And we appreciate all your help, Arellos. Thank you."

"Well, thanks...*Tom*." Arellos began walking toward the front door. "But next time you need my help, don't ask...especially if this guy is with you. Oh." Arellos snapped his fingers. "There's one other thing that may or may not be related. The Takara Dagger has been taken from a museum in Scandinavia."

Tom's eyes tightened. "The Takara Dagger?"

"Yes," Arellos said. "This dagger was given the power to destroy any living creature, including angels. I fear that someone is planning on hunting more than just deer."

"Of course, you're worried about it now." Jericho shook his head. "It can kill angels. I'm wondering if we'd be privy to this info if angels were immune."

"Sometimes I wonder why I even bother with you, Caine. If you've learned to read, there's mention of it in the book that was entrusted to you...for some unknown reason."

Arellos eyes glowed white as he glared at Jericho and walked out the door.

Jericho laughed. "I always feel so loved by those guys when they *bless* us with their presence."

Part IV

The Insurance

Jericho sat on Tom's couch and began fishing around in his duffle bag. He pulled out a freezer bag containing pieces of paper. They were brittle and faded. He carefully opened the bag and pulled out a folded piece of paper. He looked at Tom and held it out.

"And I'll assume this will explain why you're pissing off angels again?" Tom shook his head and took the paper. "I hope it's worth it."

"Just be careful opening it," Jericho said. "It's old, but it may explain this thing that's itching in the back of my brain."

Tom laughed. "Are you sure that itch isn't just because you're trying to use your brain to think for a change?"

"Ha. Ha." Jericho said sarcastically. "But if I'm right, I want you to admit that you're not the brains of this operation."

"What operation?" Tom asked. "There's no operation. Oh, let

me guess. The Death Brothers?"

"You said it, buddy." Jericho leaned back on the couch. "Just read it."

"Ok."

January 20th, 1901

To whom it may concern,

I am the assistant to Darren Frankenstein. He is trying to replicate his father's work with cellular reanimation. He has kept me at arm's length for the last week because I think he has completed his work. I followed him to a secret lab one rainy night. I couldn't enter, but I knew what was happening. Repeated lightning strikes to a tower at the top of the building let me know what he was doing. I then heard him yell, "It's alive!" several times. When he disappeared weeks later, I investigated the mostly empty lab and saw that he'd been experimenting with rats. To the common eye, no one would ever guess what he was up to. But I knew. I have no idea where Darren has fled to, but he is a dangerous man, in possession of a dangerous weapon. Please investigate.

Sincerely,

Theodore Tally

"Is this for real?" Tom asked. "There is actually a person named Frankenstein?"

Jericho sat up and reached for his beer. "You don't do your homework, Priest. It's one of the oldest stories in supernatural history. Plus, there's gotta be something in the Book of the Dead about it. It was entrusted to both us, and I entrusted it to you."

"There's not. I've checked. And do you really think the vampire siren and the missing werewolf corpse have something in common?"

"You don't?" Jericho spread out his arms. "Did you catch the part where he said, 'It's alive'? It's the same slogan the siren said was on the side of the boat that took the male siren."

"Good point." Tom walked over, took Jericho's beer, and took a sip. "But what are we missing that makes this whole thing fit together?"

"So, you're just gonna drink my beer?" Jericho glared up at Tom. "But yes. There's gotta be something that we're missing."

"First of all, big guy, I gave you the beer." Tom laughed. "Secondly, we'll figure something out on the way to the church. And thirdly, you keep calling me, Priest after you promised to stop."

Jericho sighed and stood. "So, the fate of the world hinges on a title that your father envisioned for you? He's gotta be turning over in his grave."

"My God," Tom gave the beer back to Jericho. "Have you always been a jerk?"

Jericho laughed. "Maybe."

Bristol, Rhode Island

At around noon, Wilma Trident stared out her front window as Sarah Walker walked up the steps of the front porch. The house was small, and the exterior was mostly made up of red bricks. It was in the center of the street and surrounded by a short steel fence. Sarah lived two houses down the road. She was dressed in her usual yellow housedress with pink slippers, while her hair was wrapped in a bun at the top of her head.

Wilma opened the inner white wooden door and stood at the all-screen outer door. She always wondered why she and Sarah hit it off because she was about twenty years older than Sarah. But she needed a friend, and she knew Sarah needed a friend as well.

"Hey girl," Wilma said. "I know I'm retired, but it seems like you are too."

Sarah laughed. "Yeah, yeah. I know. But when you've only been just a housewife, it's not easy finding a job when you haven't worked in ten years. Being a widow at such a young age sucks."

"Yes, I still feel sick over that." Wilma pushed open the screen door. "Well, come on in. I see you brought of your delicious pound cake."

"I think it's just ok." Sarah walked past Wilma while holding the cake with both hands. "But I appreciate the compliment."

"Either way, you're spoiling me." Wilma followed Sarah to the living room. "I'm sixty-five years old and have to keep an eye on my sugar intake."

Sarah raised her eyebrows. "I hope I look as good as you do when I reach sixty-five."

Wilma, a tall, slender woman with a mixture of blonde and gray hair, walked back into the kitchen. She grabbed two saucers, two forks, and the pitcher of coffee. She went back into the living room and sat the items on the coffee table. Then, she disappeared into the kitchen and brought back two white coffee cups.

"I could have helped you with that, Miss Wilma." Sarah reached out and took the coffee pitcher. "It's the least I could do."

"No. No." Wilma sat on the red couch next to Sarah. "I don't mind doing things for you. It makes me feel needed. Besides, you'd be around the same age as my son."

Sarah sat and took a sip of the poured coffee. "You never told me what happened to your son, Wilma."

"My son was born with a genetic disease." Tears formed in Wilma's eyes. "His father had it as well. He seemed strong and healthy until about five months after I was pregnant. He suddenly fell ill and died. When the baby was born, I was told that he'd tested positive for it. His case was more severe, and I was told he wouldn't live long after birth."

"Oh my God, Wilma. I'm so sorry."

"It's ok, honey. Either way, my son died a few days after his birth. My brother Patrick was with me to take care of my husband's arrangements, and later, my son's. I sank into a deep depression for about six months. I couldn't move. I barely ate. I didn't even attend my son's funeral." Tears streamed down her face. "I'm a terrible person, Sarah. And that's why I'm all alone now."

Sarah leaned over and hugged Wilma. "Jesus, Wilma. I am so sorry to make you relive that. What can I do?"

Wilma stood. "I'm sorry to have shared that with you, my dear…especially after what you've gone through. I'll be back."

Wilma walked down the hall and into the bathroom. She gently closed the door and leaned against it with her back. She dropped her head and wept. She began to breathe heavily. Just thinking back, remembering how she'd lost her husband and newborn baby to the same disease, brought back the guilt she felt for not going to her son's funeral. She knew her brother Patrick was being strong for them both. The Tridents had a history of having inner strength and realized that she didn't have any.

Wilma rapidly shook her head to move on. She counted to ten, breathed in and out deeply and slowly, just as the psychologist had instructed her. She then made up her mind that it was time to go back to Allentown, Rhode Island, and confront her past. It was time to find her brother Patrick and thank him for helping out all those years ago.

Wilma wiped her eyes again as she made her way back to the living room. "Thank you, Sarah. I needed that. I'm going to go back home and find my brother."

"Are you sure?" Sarah stood. "Do you need some company? I'm not doing anything right now."

"You know what, young lady?" Wilma nodded. "That's a great idea. You'll need to pack for a few days stay. I'll meet you at my car in an hour."

"Wow." Sarah clapped once. "I'm honored that you would let me tag along with you on this."

"Don't thank me yet," Wilma said. "I may just be going on a wild goose hunt. It's been thirty-five years since I left."

San Diego, California

Thaden walked into the hospital room and stood over the unconscious female patient lying in bed. She was Asian, and her hair was long. She had oxygen tubes in her nose and patches attached to both sides of her head to study her brain waves. The entire wall of windows allowed the sun to shine brightly throughout the room.

"Well, let's get this over with." Thaden took off the patches from the woman's head. "You are worth more in New York than you will ever be here."

"I'd beg to differ," A voice said from behind Thaden. "She looks just fine right where she is."

Thaden whipped around quickly. "And who are you?"

"The name's Alexander Merryweather." Alexander stood from a chair in the corner. "And now that we've gotten that out of the way, I'll pose the same question to you."

"Ahh, the wizard." Thaden tilted his head to the side. "I was wondering who was watching over Ms. Taki."

"I'm feeling a little awkward knowing that you know who I am." Alexander held out his hand, and his long white wizard's staff

56

appeared in it. "And of course, someone is watching over her. This hospital was equipped with a supernatural silent alarm system. The moment you entered, a signal was sent to my phone. I mean, you don't put an end to as many demons and the like as Ms. Taki has, and *not* made a few enemies."

"And so, you are her protector and not the priest?"

"Again," Alexander frowned. "Your knowledge of us is worrisome. But let's just say that I can get here faster."

"It's not a good day to be you, then, wizard."

Thaden charged Alexander, and they crashed into the sink behind Alexander, who dropped his staff. Thaden grabbed Alexander in a bear-hug and began to squeeze. Alexander fought to get loose. Thaden's vampire teeth appeared as he attempted to bite Alexander's neck. But Alexander head-butted Thaden and sent him stumbling backward.

"A vampire?" Alexander picked up his staff. "I was wondering when you'd reveal what you were."

"I'm not just some vampire," Thaden said.

Thaden shook off the effects of the head butt, and the vampire's teeth disappeared. They were replaced by sharp canine teeth. Fur covered the left arm of his body. He leaped across the room before Alexander could react and backhanded the wizard. Alexander fell to the floor in front of the room door. His face turned red as he grabbed his chin.

"What are you?" Alexander asked as he got back to his feet. "Some kind of hybrid creature?"

"I'm more than that." Thaden used his speed to run over, grab Alexander by the throat, and tossed the wizard across the room. "As you will find out the hard way."

Alexander fell over the medical equipment and landed on his back on the floor. He got up and looked for his staff. Before he could turn his attention back to his foe, Alexander was kicked in the face by Thaden's black boot. Alexander fell backward and hit the back of his head on the radiator. *He's fast and I'm losing. I've gotta go on the offensive, or Ms. Taki and I are doomed.* Alexander tried to shake off the blow and rise again, but Thaden ran over and kicked him in the stomach. Alexander doubled over. Thaden picked the wizard up and pressed him over his head. Blood dripped from the corner of Alexander's lip as Thaden prepared to toss Alexander out the window.

"Goodbye, wizard," Thaden said. "I can't say how much fun this has been."

Alexander held out his hand as he spotted his staff on the floor. "Revertetur ad me (return to me)."

Alexander's staff shot over to his hand. He popped Thaden in the side of the head. Thaden dropped Alexander to the floor as the monster fell to one knee. They both were drowsy as they recovered to their feet.

Thaden launched himself at Alexander. "You wretched wizard."

"Pulsus! (Pulse)." Alexander quickly said as he held up his staff.

An invisible force smashed into Thaden's chest, sending the creature crashing into the wall. He slid down to the floor and left a dent in the wall. Thaden's red eyes rolled back and then returned to normal. He frowned as he stared at Alexander, and then he took a quick glance over at Susie, who was still resting peacefully.

Thaden slowly made a motion toward her bed. "I'm not here for this."

Alexander pointed his staff at Thaden again. "Turbinis vasti (tornado)."

A breeze picked up, and a small tornado formed in the center of the room. Alexander ran over, and dove on top of Susie as adrift items in the room were sucked up in the tornado. The window broke. Thaden's feet were lifted off the floor, so he grabbed the window ledge. Alexander's eyes glowed white, and the tornado hovered over and surrounded Thaden's body. It forced his hand to be snatched away from the metal ledge, taking a chunk of it with him.

"T-This isn't o-over, wizard," Thaden said.

Alexander flicked his wrist. "For now, yes, it is."

The tornado escaped out of the window and took Thaden with it. Alexander got up and looked down at Susie. She was still out. He walked past the still falling debris to look out the window. He watched as the tornado carried Thaden away until he was out of sight.

Alexander breathed heavily and bent over. He rested his hands on his knees. He was startled as two hospital guards burst into the room with their guns drawn.

"Freeze," the guard in front said. "Put your hands over your head."

"I'm too tired, guys." Alexander straightened up. "I've just done your job. Now, go get the doctors to come check on Ms. Taki."

The guards looked at each other with confused expressions on their faces. They put their guns back in their holsters. They nodded at Alexander and put their weapons back in the holsters.

"We know who you are, Mr. Merryweather," one guard said. "We'll go get the doctor."

The guards exited. Alexander surveyed the room, which was in shambles. *Susie is safe for now. That's all a care about. Now, I've got to find out what that thing was.*

Part V

The Takara Dagger

Denmark, Scandinavia

A tall, slender man with a brunette buzz cut walked toward the warehouse entrance. It was almost midnight. He was well-built and had two healed welts on the left side of his face. Lights shined on the building from the ground, and a line of women in sparkling dresses and men in tuxedos lined up at the entrance as well. The man, Olaf Sader, upon entering the building, grabbed a glass of Champagne from the waiter. He sipped it and surveyed the guests in the room. He recognized a few, but he chose not to converse with any of them.

"Mr. Sader," a short, almost bald white man stuck out his pudgy hand to shake and began to speak in Danish. "I wondered if I'd recognize anyone else here."

"That's funny," Olaf said, as he spoke in Danish and ignored the man's hand. "I was hoping I didn't run into anyone that I knew.

Pity."

"Why, pity?" The man asked

"Because I'm gonna have to do this." Olaf turned to walk away. "Good day."

Olaf looked around the room at the swank cars on private stages and weaponry in glass containers. The auction only attracted the wealthy. But it also attracted others…those who frequented black market gatherings.

After taking stock of the entire showroom, Olaf found his seat in the front row. *I should have known it wouldn't be on display out in the open. But I didn't know extra security would be here.* Those thoughts rolled through Olaf's head as he watched five heavily armed guards, in matching grey uniforms, waiting near the back entrance.

He reached in his inner shirt pocket and pulled out white cigarette rolling papers. He reached in his front pants pocket and pulled out a small bag of tobacco. The lights were dimmed as he continued to roll. Red lights then lit up the place, and a spotlight shined on the stage in front of Olaf. He licked the rolled the cigarette, pulled out a lighter, and lit it.

An older man with gray hair and matching beard walked onto the stage and stood behind the podium. "Welcome to the annual Denmark Auction, the pride of Scandinavia. We will start with our least expensive items. So, of course, we'll be starting with cars."

Olaf waited. Others roamed around to get food or more to drink, but he didn't budge. He waited for two hours and smoked at least ten hand-rolled cigarettes. The host waved to the guards, and they brought out two glass cases. One held a battle-ax, and the other held a golden dagger. The dagger was the length as an adult arm, and its sharpened edges glistened off the overhead lights.

The host stepped up to the podium again. "And now, we have, what I'll assume most of you have been waiting for..." He held out his hand and gestured toward the glass cases. "... here we have the famous battle-ax of one of Heaven's most fierce warriors...the Bad Angel. He used this ax in the Great War in Heaven and two wars here on earth against the underworld. It is safe to say that this weapon has seen more action than any weapon besides the flaming sword. It was recovered in the aftermath of the battle in Las Vegas."

The crowd gasped. Ushers walked around and replaced the ordering paddles with another paddle. One side was red and the other one blue. The red side represented fifty million dollars, and the blue side represented one hundred million dollars. Only five paddles were handed out. Most people remaining had already purchased what they'd come for. The others were the high-rollers.

"I will start the bidding at five hundred million dollars," the host said.

"How did you come to have such a thing?" A woman dressed in black and wearing a black vale asked. "No human can wield an angel's weapon."

The host smiled. "It was stumbled upon by a wanderer in the Nevada desert. I didn't ask how we came to have it. And no one is saying you have to wield it. Just having it is the prize."

The woman nodded her head, as the other guests did. Everyone stood except for Olaf. A skinny observer leaned over Olaf's shoulder and knocked the cigarette out of his hand. Olaf looked back at the man, who apologized, but he didn't care as he elbowed the man in the groin. The man fell backward, and another person took his place.

The ax sold for eight hundred million dollars. The guards rolled the next item to the podium. They stepped off the stage and stood in front of the platform with their hands on their weapons. Olaf dropped his cigarette and stepped on it. He was one of the five people who'd received a paddle.

The smile returned to the host's face. "Our last item of the night is the best. It is known as the Takara Dagger. No one truly knows everything that it is capable of. But one thing we surely do know is that it can kill any living thing, including angels and demons."

Gasps again rang out throughout the warehouse. Everyone stood up, including Olaf. It was what he'd been waiting for. He patted the paddled on his thigh looked around to study the others who held a paddle.

"I will start the bidding at one billion," the host said.

Three of the paddle holders dropped their paddles except for Olaf and a young woman. She wore sunglasses and a white dress. She was tall, long black hair with tanned skin and bright red lipstick. She looked over at Olaf as well and stared at him from over her sunglasses.

Olaf held up his one hundred-million-dollar paddle.

"One point one billion," the host said. "Do I hear more?"

"Two billion." The woman raised her paddle and looked at Olaf. "Beat that."

Olaf dropped his paddle. He was willing to go to one-point-five billion, but that was it. The host asked for higher bids three times, and no one else made a move.

"Sold! To the young lady to my right." The host pointed to her. "Enjoy your purchases, ladies, and gentlemen. And goodnight."

Looks like I'll just have to get the dagger by other means. Olaf turned to walk away. He glanced one last time at the young woman, who was shaking hands with the people next to her.

Olaf walked out with a disappointed expression on his face. The valet pulled up and gave him the keys to his black, two-door, sport's car. He drove a half-mile down the road and pulled to the side away from traffic. He cut off his headlights and waited. He turned and pulled out binoculars. He watched as the young woman walked out with five guards in black suits surrounding her. They got into two black SUVs and drove to the back of the warehouse, where Olaf assumed they were loading the dagger. He rolled another cigarette and waited.

New York

The phone rang, but no one answered. It rang again just as Tom walked through the front door of his apartment. *Dammit. I'll bet its Caine still laughing at his little joke from earlier. I should just let it ring.* Tom walked faster. He didn't like it when Jericho made fun of his attire, but the slayer mostly made Tom laughed.

Tom sighed as he picked up the phone, "Yeah. What is it now?"

"Excuse me?"

"Caine?"

"No. This is Alexander."

"Oh. I'm sorry about that, Alexander." Tom's forehead creased. "I thought you were Caine. But what's up?"

"It's Susie."

Tom dropped the phone to the floor. He put his hands on his hips and stared out the window. He thought about the last time he saw Susan when he flew her unconscious body back to San Diego to be near her family. She looked so peaceful lying in the hospital bed. He then remembered when he asked Alexander to check on Susie every so often after they installed the supernatural detector at the hospital. Tom snapped out of his trance as he heard Alexander speaking louder into the phone. Tom picked up the phone again.

"Thomas, dammit. Are you still there?"

"Sorry about that, Alexander. What happened? Is she awake?"

"No. No. It's not that. We had a visitor yesterday."

"A visitor?" Tom stroked his furrowed brow. "Who?"

"He was some kind of hybrid. A vampire and werewolf."

"That's impossible. They *don't* exist."

"This one does. He was talking about taking Susie back to New York."

"Really?" Tom dropped his head to think and still listen to Alexander. "Did he give his name?"

"Yes. Thaden, I think."

"Thaden. He's a vampire siren that was taken hostage. Well, he's a vampire, alright. I just don't know why he'd been going after Susie. Just keep an eye on her a little longer, would you?"

"Of course, Tom. What will you do?"

"I'm going to get in contact with Caine to see if he's heard something about your visitor. And Alexander?"

"Yeah, Thomas."

"Thank you. I'm sure the encounter wasn't peaceful."

"Thanks. Be careful."

Tom hit a button on the phone to end the call. Once he heard dial tone again, he punched in Jericho's pager number. He asked the slayer to get in contact as soon as possible. Tom sat on the couch, and the back of his foot continuously tapped the floor. He noticed it and grab his leg with both hands to stop it. He stared at the TV, which was turned off. *What does Susie have to do with all this? She's been in a coma for almost a month.*

Tom let his thoughts drift. He remembered the battle with

Ahmya Taki, Susie's aunt. She was a powerful witch who showed Susie how to use her powers. However, Ahmya was in league with the demon lord, Hangoctuforre, and she asked Susie to kill Tom. Susie refused, which led to the fight that Susie killed her aunt. However, it left Susie in a coma.

As Tom sat on the couch, tears weld up in his eyes. Susie had sacrificed herself to save him, and he wanted to do the same for her. The phone rang, and Tom snapped out of his trance again.

"Hello?"

"Hey, Priest. It's Jericho. What's going on?"

"Caine, it seems that our missing vampire siren has shown up...in San Diego of all places."

"What was he doing there?"

"According to the wizard, he showed up to the hospital for Susie. He was trying to bring her back here to New York?"

"Is she awake? And New York? What the hell for?"

"No. She's still in a coma. But I'm confused as well. I don't know what our next play should be. So, I told Alexander to sit tight until I contacted you."

"Hmm. The way I see it is, you have only two choices. Continue to let the wizard protect her or bring her here, and we can all do it together."

"I promised Alexander that we wouldn't call on him again until your pal, the Hangman, resurfaced. He's got newborns to tend to."

Jericho sighed. "Right. I say, let's go bring her here and cut the wizard loose. He doesn't need any more distractions."

"Wow, Caine. I'm surprised that you care."

"Ha. Ha. Ha. I don't. Seems like there will be some action involved. Why should we let the wizard have all the fun?"

Tom shook his head. "I should have known."

Tom hung up the phone and went into his bedroom. He didn't use it often, but he had a laptop on his nightstand. He opened it and began searching for plane tickets for him and Jericho. He knew they'd have to use military planes to escort them back. But after the fight in the Nevada desert, he felt that the government owed them for saving the world again. *I don't remember Susie mentioning anything about a run-in with vampires, especially sirens. I guess we'll figure it out once we get her back here. This should be simple. Hopefully, Caine won't do anything to make this harder than it has to be.*

Denmark, Scandinavia

Olaf followed the two black SUVs to a huge white house just outside the city. There was a twenty-foot high brick wall that surrounded the estate. A secured black metal gate was upfront, so he stopped on the dirt road leading to the driveway. He opened his trunk and pulled out a leather-covered briefcase. He opened it and smiled as the moonlight made the contents sparkle. There were two forty-five gold plated revolvers, a switchblade with a black handle, and black leather pants, with a matching buttoned-down shirt. He picked up a backpack, which held more equipment.

He took off the tuxedo shirt and put on the leather shirt. He put the brown leather holsters around his waist and placed the guns in the holster. He put the knife in its ankle holster. Olaf walked toward the house. He pulled a grappling hook and rope from the backpack and threw it over the wall. He heard what sounded like several dogs on the other side. *Damn. They would have to have dogs too. I hate dogs. But luckily, I came prepared.*

Olaf reached into his backpack again and pulled out two freezer bags containing raw steaks. He climbed up the wall and looked over where he saw three dogs barking at him. He tossed the steaks to the ground in front of the dogs and watched them devour them. He knew the steaks wouldn't distract the dogs for long, so he reached into his backpack and pulled out the tranquilizer clip for his guns. He loaded the clip and shot the dogs on their sides. He waited on top of the wall until the dogs passed out.

Olaf jumped to the ground and tipped pass the dogs. He then sprinted to the house. The guards were still inside: they had a live-in house to the right of the main house. He watched as three of the five guards went into the guardhouse, and the other two patrolled the grounds.

"I don't hear the dogs," the short-haired blond guard said. "Where do you think they are?"

"Let's go out back and see if they are asleep." The brunette guard swung the strap of his AK-47 over his shoulder. "They usually bark at everything, including us."

Olaf hid behind the white fountain statue in front of the house

70

until the guards walked around back. He tipped up to the front door, which was unlocked. He walked in. Most of the lights were out. *Now, where would they put such a precious artifact? I'll check the cellar first.*

Olaf crept down the stairs to the wine cellar. There were seven rows of wine shelves, each holding about twenty bottles, and the walls were metal. Only one was wooden, which made Olaf focus on it more. *Something's off about that wall.* The wooden wall had tiles throughout. Olaf pulled out a pen. He clicked the top of it, and a red pointer light shined on the wall. If the wall were solid, the light would remain red. However, the light turned green and stayed green as he glided the pen across the entire wall. *Just as I thought.*

Olaf pressed on each of the tiles on the wall. He pushed on a tile near the floor, and it sank in, causing the wall the slide up. A bright light popped on from a room that was behind the wall. It contained shelves with gold bars and money in different dominations. In the back, still in its glass casing, was the Takara Dagger.

Suddenly, an alarm sounded along with flashing red lights throughout the wine cellar. *So much for doing this quietly.* Olaf pulled out one of his guns and shot, shattering the glass casing. He pulled out the dagger and put it in a backpack. He ran toward the door. On his way up the stairs, the two guards ran down and started shooting. Olaf pulled out his pistols and shot once from each gun. The shots hit the guards in the middle of their foreheads. Olaf stepped to the side and continued up the stairs as the guards tumbled past him. When he got to the top, the other three guards had just entered the house, each armed with AK-47's as well.

They turned over the couch and wooden table and started a firefight. Olaf dove behind a brick table, where a portrait of the young woman's family was. He turned it over but didn't fire. He waited until the guards stopped firing and looked out when the smoke cleared. One of the guards was in sight; the other two still hid behind the table. Olaf shot. Another direct hit in the head. The guard collapsed to the floor, then, the other two opened fire again. Olaf looked to his left. A rounding staircase leading to the second floor was there. He reached into his backpack and grabbed a grenade. He threw it at the guards, and it exploded. However, it was as a smoke grenade, of which Olaf used as a distraction to run up the stairs.

As Olaf made his way down the hall once he reached the top, he could hear the guards making their way up the stairs. He kicked open the two white double doors at the end of the hall. He ducked as soon as he entered. A baseball bat was swung at his head. It was the young lady dressed in a pink nightgown. Olaf recovered and punched her in the jaw. She fell to the floor, but Olaf immediately picked her up, stood behind her, and put his arm around her neck.

"Close the door." He pushed her from behind until she closed both doors. "You're gonna help me get out of here."

"You don't know what you're doing," she said. "I recognize you from the auction. I'll assume you have the dagger in your bag. I was buying it for someone that you don't want to steal from."

"Who?" Olaf asked.

"She was an angel."

"Why would an angel use a human to get the dagger? They would simply just need to take it."

"That's the thing." She struggled to move his arm so she could breathe. "They can't even touch the dagger."

"What?"

Before she could speak again, the doors were kicked in. The two guards pointed their guns at Olaf and the woman. They then cut on their sniper lasers and aimed them at Olaf's head.

"Let her go, scum," One guard said.

"You guys have just screwed up," Olaf replied

The other guard laughed. "How? We've got you cold. You're not leaving this room alive."

"You should have just entered the room and opened fire." Olaf walked backward to the window, still holding the woman. "Because I don't need a laser."

The two guards looked at each other with confused expressions on their faces. Olaf shot the one on the right in the head, who fell backward to his death. Olaf then dove out of the window. He twisted his body to fire his gun as he and the girl fell. The other guard ran over to the window and was met by a bullet to the head as well. Olaf shifted his body in the air again, just in time to land on top of the young woman as they hit the ground. She cracked her head on the concrete below and died almost instantly.

Olaf got up and shook his head rapidly. He put his pistol back in the holster and dusted off his clothes. He began to walk and realized he hurt his knee during the fall. He limped toward the front gate.

A dog attacked from the left and pushed Olaf to the ground. Saliva dripped from the dog's mouth as he tried to bite Olaf in the face, but Olaf held the dog by the throat. Olaf couldn't reach his pistols. However, as he kicked his legs in the air, his switchblade fell out to the ground. He grabbed the knife and stabbed the dog. The dog continued to try to bite Olaf until it rolled over and died. Olaf stood and limped toward the gate again, but the other dogs charged toward him. *I don't' have time for this crap.* Olaf pulled out his pistols and shot the dogs in the head.

Olaf made it to his car. He tossed his backpack in the passenger seat. He breathed in and let out a deep sigh, just before starting the car and pulled off. *That was interesting information. I think my asking price has just increased.*

Downtown New York

Thaden exited the penthouse elevator. He stopped and looked around as the lights were out, and it was quiet. *I need minions. I need people to rejoice when I enter a room. To run up to me and bow down.* The lights cut on, and Dr. Ranken entered from the swinging dining-room door.

"How was San Diego?" Dr. Ranken asked.

"I ran into a slight problem," Thaden said. "The wizard was there."

"Really? How was that experience?"

"Interesting. I realized that I'll need something extra, though."

Dr. Ranken motioned to the swinging door. "How's about these guys?"

Five men entered the room, dressed in new all-black suits. Thaden sniffed the air and smiled.

"Vampires." Thaden nodded. "Is this all?"

"There are ten more assets – well, the best way to describe them is the walking dead. They are in the basement. They prefer it down there in the dark."

"Are they loyal to our cause?"

"There's only one that talks," Dr. Ranken said. "If you can call it that. He is also the only one that can think for himself. The others are loyal to him. But *he* is loyal to us, thanks to our angel partner."

"Great." Thaden clasped his hands together. "It's not the army I expected, but they will suffice. Five vampires and ten – whatever. I still need something that gives me a more of personal advantage."

"Well, I think we've acquired just what you need." Dr. Ranken sat on the couch. "I've just received a call from our Scandinavian asset. He's acquired the prize."

"Good. When can we take possession of it?"

"That's the thing. His asking price has gone up?"

"What does he want?"

"What all men want…power."

"Soon, we'll have plenty, so that won't be a problem. Reach out to him again and tell him to hurry. Once we have it, there won't be anyone, man or supernatural, that can stop us."

Part VI

The Awakening

New York Memorial Hospital

Tom picked up the pace as the doctor and nurses pushed the gurney down the hall. They'd told Tom to stay back, so he tried to comply as much as he could. Susie had been plugged back to the machines that monitored her vitals, but Tom wanted to be sure she was okay. It was just a matter of getting her to a comfortable room. The flight was a little over six hours, and he had to make sure she was ok. He'd promised her parents she'd be ok, as a condition for them agreeing to let Tom take her.

He sat in the waiting room as instructed and sipped coffee. He didn't usually drink that beverage, but he hadn't gotten much rest since he awoke that day and boarded the plane to New York. *I'll assume Thaden wanted to use her to keep me in line. I don't know what I would do if something terrible were to happen to her because of me.*

The doctor came out. He was a young brunette with brown eyes and a clean-shaven; he was wearing a white jacket over blue scrubs. He smiled as he approached Tom in which Tom took as a good sign.

"My name is Doctor Walker, Mr. Padilla," the doctor said. "Her vitals are normal. And after looking at the doctor's notes from San Diego, everything appears to be ok."

Tom let out a deep exhale. "Thanks, doc. I didn't know how big of a risk it would be to transport her across the country."

"I understand." Dr. Walker gestured toward the hall. "Walk with me. We've just received the paperwork from her family that grants you power of attorney. You can go see her if you want."

"Yes, I want to see her," Tom said as he shook the young doctor's hand. "Anything new you can tell me about the coma?"

Dr. Walker sighed. "Sorry. Unfortunately, that prognosis is unchanged as well."

Tom thanked the doctor and went inside Susie's room. He walked over, sat in the green recliner next to her bed, held her hand, and just stared her face. *She looks so peaceful. Still the beautiful woman I fell in love with. She's is what makes all this craziness worth-while.*

Tom sat back in the chair to relax. He turned his head slightly toward the window as he heard thunder. *That's weird. I hadn't noticed how those pink clouds have hovered closer to the ground.* Tom stood and walked toward the window. He placed his hand on his hips and stared out at the city.

Allentown, Rhode Island

The red rental car pulled up to the secluded house on the outskirts of town. Acres of land stretched in each direction before other houses could be seen. The windows were boarded, and the white paint was faded and worn. The fence surrounding the house was mostly rusted, and there were no gate doors on the fence.

"Should we keep going?" Sarah said as he drummed the steering wheel with her thumb. "It's definitely abandoned. Doesn't look like anyone has lived here in quite some time." "Yeah," Wilma began. "Drive up to the front porch. I'd like to get a closer look."

They drove toward the house. Wilma leaned over to look outside the window: she saw the family graves in the backyard from a distance. Her heart beat faster, and she began to sweat. Her stomach started to churn. She put her hand over her heart as her eyes watered.

"Oh my God, Wilma." Sarah pressed the brake to slow down. "Are you okay? Do you want to stop?"

"No. Don't stop. I just had a sinking feeling in my stomach, is all."

They pulled up to the front porch and got out. Wilma looked around. The grass was dead, and only a few trees remained. She took a step to walk up the stairs and stopped. She leaned to the side to look at the back of the house and decided to head to the backyard. As she passed the side door, a memory flashed through her head. It was the night she was in labor, and her brother rushed her out of the side door to get into the car. They were headed to the hospital.

As they got to the back yard, Wilma's pace slowed. There were three headstones in front of an old apple tree. Surprisingly, huge red apples bloomed from the tree. She walked over and passed the first two headstones. She knew they belonged to parents, Trevor, and Kara Trident, who'd died before she left Allentown. *This third one has to be my baby boy.* She finally burst into tears. *What am I doing here? I don't even know my son's name.*

She knelt in front of the headstone and began to brush off the dirt that had obscured the engraving. Her eyes popped open when she finally read what it said. *Patrick? But how? When?* She finished brushing off the dirt and saw that he'd died fifteen years prior.

"I'm sorry, Wilma." Sara walked over and put her hand on Wilma's shoulder. "I can't imagine how you must feel right now."

"I-I can't believe it." Wilma wiped the tears from her eyes. "My whole family is right here."

"I'll give you some time by yourself." Sarah squeezed Wilma's shoulder. "I'll go see if I can get inside the house. Maybe there's something inside that can help explain things."

Sarah walked away and disappeared around the corner. Wilma sat with her back up against Patrick's headstone and held her head. She then wondered where her son was laid to rest. *Could Patrick have buried him next to his father at the cemetery? I must know. It's the only way I'm going to get over all of this.*

Part VI: The Awakening

Wilma stood and dusted off her pants. She looked toward the house and wondered how Sarah was going to get in. She walked back around the front of the house, but she didn't see Sarah. The windows and front door were still boarded. She put her hands on her hips and stared at the house from top to bottom. Suddenly, she heard a noise from the other side of the house. She walked over and saw Sarah standing inside at a window.

"There was no board?" Wilma asked.

"Nope," Sarah responded. "Now, here, give me your hand."

Sarah held Wilma's hand as she stepped inside the house. The window was at the top of the basement stairs, while a door was to the right of the window. Wilma decided to go check out the rest of the house instead of going down to the basement.

"No," Sarah said as he pulled Wilma back from opening the door. "I've already checked upstairs. It's empty. Let's go down."

Wilma's eyes tightened. "Oh. Ok."

The two women walked down the stairs and stopped as the daylight gave way to the darkness in the basement.

"Luckily, I came prepared." Sarah opened her purse, pulled out, and cut on a flashlight. "You never know when you're going to need something like this."

"Wow," Wilma began. "You're like my personal Indiana Jones. You really know your way around in the dark."

"Yeah, it's what happens when your husband worked all day and left you alone in a huge house."

"Apparently."

Wilma followed Sarah around the basement. They searched the two empty rooms and then went back out to the family room, where Sarah shined the flashlight on a box in the farthest corner. It was the only thing in the room.

"Wait," Wilma said. "Shine the light on the wall again."

Sarah shone the light just above the box. Carved in the wall were the words *Jericho C. Roberts was here.* A few inches to the right, *Jericho Caine was here*, was also carved into the wall.

"Roberts." Wilma pondered. "That was my late husband's last name. But I don't know any Jericho *C.* Roberts…or Jericho Caine. Jericho's middle name was Franklin."

"Maybe these two Jericho's are the same person," Sarah responded.

Wilma bent and picked up the light box with both hands. "Let's go," Wilma said. "There's nothing else here."

"Agreed."

Wilma followed Sarah back up the stairs to the open window. Sarah climbed out first. However, Wilma opened and looked out the door. The door led to the kitchen. Small amounts of little light shined through the small cracks in the windows. The house was empty, just as Sarah had said. However, Wilma looked down and saw wooden boards on the floor. *Hmm. Wouldn't the boards be on the outside of the house instead of the inside, if someone had taken them down? That's odd.*

"Are you coming, Wilma?"

"Y-yes. Right behind you."

Wilma ducked and stepped outside the window. "Sorry about that. I was daydreaming."

"Don't worry," Sarah said. "I totally understand."

Sarah led the way as they headed back to the front of the house. Wilma turned back around and looked at the window as they just left. The paint around the edges of the window was lighter than the rest of the house. *Looks like the wood covering was just recently taken down.*

Sarah drove, and Wilma sat on the passenger seat of the car as they headed back to their hotel. Wilma rummaged through the box and pulled out two photo albums. Wilma flipped through the first album. There were pictures of her and the Trident family from when she was a child. The other photo album had pictures of her and her brother Patrick as young adults. She smiled as she enjoyed the older photos from past birthdays. She placed the box on the car floor and then noticed a small wallet-sized picture in the box. It was newer. She picked it up and saw two men standing side by side. They had smiles on their faces with an arm draped across each other's back. They were dressed in black and green army fatigues.

"Pull over!" Wilma barked and startled Sarah. "Pull over!"

"Why? What is it, Wilma?"

"This can't be." Wilma shook her head. "Jericho was never in the army."

"Are you sure it's him?" Sarah pulled over to the side of the road and cut on the emergency lights. "Could it be someone who looks like him?"

"This looks exactly like him, though, except a little more muscular."

Wilma flipped the photo over to the back. *Jericho and Randolph* were written in blue ink. Wilma stared out the window. Her eyes tightened. She'd never known anyone name Randolph either. Wilma then stared down at the picture again. *What's going on here? On second thought, he looks almost exactly like Jericho, but it's not him. Jericho didn't have a scar over his right eye.*

Sarah squeezed Wilma's arm. "What do you want to do, Wilma? Are you ok? Because you look like you've seen a ghost."

Wilma peered into Sarah's face. "Not a ghost. But maybe something else. Let's go back to the hotel. I need to use a computer."

Wilma rushed through the hotel lobby with Sarah in tow. Wilma glared into each room she walked by until she found the one she sought. It was the business room. She walked in, and she immediately noticed that the room was small. Three computers sat table across the room, and a fax machine was off to the right.

She pulled out one of the chairs and sat. She moved the mouse, and the black screen came alive. She clicked on the icon for the internet. She typed *Jericho Caine* into the search engine, and her mouth fell open. She put her hand over her heart as she watched the screen fill up with countless stories, pictures, and videos. *Oh my God. Where have I been when all this happened? How did I not know about this?*

"I'm not the smartest person in the world, Wilma," Sarah said as she peered over Wilma's shoulder. "But, I'm starting to think that Jericho Caine is your son."

"But this can't be." Wilma teared up. "Why would Patrick not tell me?"

"It seems obvious that Jericho doesn't know about you, Wilma. Who knows what he believes happened to you all those years ago."

"These clips and articles only talk about what happened in Las Vegas. It doesn't say why he was there. It doesn't say where he lives or how to get in touch with him."

Sarah crossed her arms. "Hmm. Leave that to me. My husband was a realtor. Maybe I can use some of his old contacts to find out *something*."

Wilma stood and hugged Sarah. "But you've done so much already. Are you sure?"

"Anything for you, Miss Wilma."

Later That Night

Jericho knocked on the hotel room door. He leaned up against the wall and drummed it with his fingers. He stared at the ground as he heard noises from inside.

"Just a minute." A female's voice rang out.

Jericho stood back from the door. He wanted to take in the entire scene, and whoever answered the door. The door opened with Wilma standing there, a huge smile on her face. Her eyes were glazed as she cuffed her hands over her nose and mouth.

"My God," she said. "You look just like him."

Jericho smiled. "You must be Wilma?"

"Yes, son. I'm your mother."

Wilma spread out her arms and walked toward Jericho. He took a step forward and hugged her: squeezing tighter, she rested her head on his shoulder. She began to cry and rubbed his back.

"I can't believe this." Wilma took a step backward and eyed Jericho from head to toe. "You're so big, son."

"I work out." Jericho grinned. "May I come in?"

"Oh, of course. I'm so shocked that I've lost my manners."

"Don't worry, Wilma. I think I'm feeling the same way."

Jericho followed Wilma into the room. He pulled out the leather chair from the round table next to the huge window. Wilma sat on one of the two queen-sized beds.

"I have some bottled water," she said as he pointed to the small refrigerator. "It's not that cold, though."

"I'm fine," Jericho replied. "If I may ask. Where have you been, Wilma? And how did you find me?"

"Luck, and a little help from a friend. After I was told you died, son, I fell into a deep depression and moved away. Why didn't Pat tell me you were alive?"

Jericho stared off to the wall. "I think for two reasons. One, I think you were still emotionally too fragile. Then as time went on, Uncle Pat began to believe I was different, which coincided with the mission he was charged with."

Wilma sighed. "Not that business about the 'one true

slayer'?"

"You know about that?"

"Come on, son. I'm a Trident. That's all we heard about for years from our father when we were young. As the years came and went, we heard less and less about it. Are you saying that *you are him*?"

"Yes." Jericho leaned forward and rested his forearms on his knees. "Uncle Pat said that you never believed in the story. He mentioned that you didn't want any part of the Trident's legacy."

Wilma slowly shook her head. "I'm so sorry, son. But I think Pat may have been right. I was so messed up over losing you and your father. I probably couldn't have dealt with knowing you were alive after being told you'd died."

"It's ok, Wilma." Jericho stood, reached out, and took Wilma's hand. "We're together now. I've turned off my pager, so we won't be disturbed. And we have plenty of time to catch – "

A knock at the door startled Jericho, who spun around quickly. He reached behind his back but realized he didn't bring his sword.

"It's ok." Wilma stood and grabbed Jericho's arm. "It's just my friend Sarah."

Wilma walked over and opened the door. Sarah walked in and immediately lock eyes with Jericho.

"Hi!" Sarah put out her hand to shake Jericho's. "I'm Sarah. I helped drive Wilma here."

"Thank you," Jericho replied as he shook her hand. "We can

never repay you."

Wilma cleared her throat and smiled. "I think you can, son. Wilma is single. She would like to have a night out in town before we leave."

"Miss Wilma," Sarah blushed. "You're embarrassing me."

"What about us?" Jericho asked. "I was hoping to use this time to get to know you."

"We'll have plenty of time to catch up," Wilma said. "I'm retired and can spend as much time with you as you can spare."

Jericho smiled as he glared at Sarah and then back to Wilma. "Um, ok. If you're sure, and you don't mind…"

"I don't," Wilma replied, smiling.

Downtown New York

Around midnight, Sariel landed in the alley behind the skyscraper. She scanned the area in all directions. She walked up to a metal door, yanked it off the hinges. The alarm sounded. Sariel eye's glowed white, and the alarm shut off. She looked above the door and saw a surveillance camera. Her eyes lit up again, and the camera exploded, sending sparks out in all directions. Sariel entered the building. The exit opened into a stairwell, and she walked down five stories to the basement.

When Sariel entered the boiler room, it was steamy and dark. A dim light bulb could be seen across the room on the far wall. Suddenly, a pale hand grabbed her arm. She grabbed the arm and tossed its owner across the room. Ten more pale men closed in from the shadows. They walked slowly and grunted.

"If I rip off your heads," Sariel took a step backward, "I'm told you'll be dead, and not just undead."

"Halt!" A deep voice rang out from the dark. "Who you?"

"I am the angel Sariel," she said. "And I am the reason you exist."

A pale and dirty-blonde haired man stepped out into the dim light. He dragged his left leg. He was tall, about six feet-nine inches, and weighed about two hundred pounds. Dark circles were under his eyes, and a dried black substance was under his nose.

"I am Mobus." He said. "I am boss."

"How would you like to enter into an agreement with me, Mobus?" Sariel asked as her eyes tightened from all the grunting. "I can make you a stronger boss and help you get out of this basement."

"Mobus just wants brains for them and me."

Sariel readied herself as the other pale men grew closer. "I can make you the boss of more than just these guys."

"How?" Mobus cocked his head to the side and motioned to the others. "Thaden tells me, and I tell them."

"I entered your mind before you came back to life, Mobus. I am the one who gave you power over the others—the one who gave you the ability to think and talk. I instructed you to follow Thaden. But when the time comes," she smiled. "I will give you a weapon to kill Thaden and become your own boss."

"Mobus can lead?"

"Yes." Sariel nodded. "Then you can grow your ranks and have all the brains to eat that you want. Although, I expected there to be a lot more of you than there are."

Mobus stepped aside and motioned toward the inner boiler room. "Come. Tell Mobus more, angel friend."

New York Park

Tom picked up the pace into a full sprint as he ran around the park. It was around ten o'clock in the morning, and he didn't like being around people. He didn't have an office at the church anymore, so he spent most of his days either training in hand to hand combat or working out. The park's bike and running path were perfect for him.

Tom looked down at his watch, he realized he was a couple of minutes ahead of his five-mile run. He decided to take a seat on a metal park bench. Several trees surrounded the bench and blocked out the sun. The breeze felt great as hit brushed up against his sweaty back. He was thirsty, so he waited for the local vendor to push the refreshment cart around.

Tom purchased some water and sat back on the bench. He drank almost all of the twelve-ounce beverage in one gulp. He then spread out his arm and leaned back on the bench. He knew he didn't have much time to rest as the lunch crowd would soon be out throughout the park. Plus, he wanted to go back to the hospital and sit with Susie.

He took a deep breath and exhaled. He watched the ducks play in the pond in front of him. The wind picked up, and a breeze blew by the right side of Tom's face. He turned to his right and saw Arellos standing with his hands on his hips.

"Are you following me, angel?" Tom asked.

"I like to stay in touch with friends," Arellos replied as he reached up to fix his sunglasses. "Besides, you're not with Caine, which means this conversation will go more smoothly."

Tom chuckled. "Come on. He's a good guy once you get to know him."

"I'll take your word for it." Arellos sat next to Tom. "But on to why I'm here. We have a major problem, Thomas."

Tom dropped his head and shook it. "This can't be good. You guys rarely seek us out unless it's bad news."

"It's not good."

"Well," Tom said. "Are you gonna share?"

"We've failed." Arellos ran his hand through his blond hair. "We tried to acquire the Takara Dagger before it fell into the wrong hands. Like I said, we failed."

"Who has it?"

"An assassin named Olaf Sader. He intercepted the human we used to purchase it at an underground auction."

"Why didn't one of your angels stop him?"

"It's a human affair." Arellos hunched his shoulders. "We're not allowed to interfere...even with this."

"So, where are he and the dagger now?"

"From what we've gathered, he touched down here in New

York last night. My guess is, he's gonna attempt to sell the dagger to someone here."

"And you don't know who?"

"Not yet," Arellos said. "But when I find out, you'll be the first to know."

"Oh yeah, thanks," Tom responded sarcastically. "Caine's gonna love this."

"That's why I told you, Thomas." Arellos stood. "I'll let you inform the slayer."

"Great."

Arellos looked around, spread his wings, and took off. Tom leaned back against the bench again and drank the last of his water. *If the angels are worried, this must be important. I've got to get ready. If the dagger is as dangerous as he says, no one is safe.*

Tom stood and began to walk back to his apartment. He had to page Jericho so they could go after the dagger. He hated to admit it to himself, but fighting humans was his weakness. *I can match the power of any demon I face. When plain ole humans are involved, things become complicated. If I encounter the dagger, Jericho's Sword of Caine may be our best option.*

Tom showered and put on his traditional all-black clothes. He put hair gel in his hair and combed it until it was slicked back like he liked. He paged Jericho before he got in the shower, and the slayer hadn't returned his call. Neither had cell phones, and neither the man understood why. Either way, Jericho wasn't responding.

Ok, that's it. I know I gave the wizard my word, but it looks like I may have to break it if Caine doesn't respond.

Tom sat on the couch next to his phone, which sat in the in-table. He put his pager on the coffee table in front of him and waited. He shook his head several times as he folded his arms and frowned. *Dammit, Jericho. Where the hell are you?*

Tom got up and paced. He continuously stared down as his pager, but nothing happened. *Screw this!* He finally went into his bedroom. He knelt in front of his bed, reached under it, and pulled out a black trunk. He wasn't sure if he should gather his demon-hunting weapons, as he was sure he'd be confronting normal humans. Either way, he put a brass knuckle in each of his jacket pockets. He pulled out his silver metallic pole and slid it in its holster, which was strapped to his leg.

Tom was ready. He walked back out to his living room and was startled by a visitor. He stuck his hand in his pockets and slipped on his brass knuckles.

"Hold on, Thomas." Arellos put out his hands. "It's just me."

"Jesus, Arellos." Tom put the weapons back in his pockets. "Please, don't do that again."

"Sorry, Priest. But I have news."

"I'm not a priest."

"Sorry. I keep forgetting." Arellos smiled. "But I have a lead on the dagger." He handed Tom a piece of paper. "I have it on good authority that it will be at this address later today."

"And let me guess," Tom began. "It's still a human matter, so you won't be able to help."

"See." Arellos patted Tom on the shoulder. "You're learning."

"Yeah. Yeah. Yeah."

Allentown, Rhode Island

Jericho pulled out a chair and slid it back as Sarah sat. They were at a local restaurant called Marcy's Café. It was small and could hold about twenty patrons. Less than that were there that night. They sat at a round table with two chairs. Near them, there was a bar, where a few people were seated and watched four flat-screen televisions, which were placed just above the liquor bottles. A jukebox sat in the far corner and played songs automatically.

Sarah wore a sundress, which was red, with yellow sunflowers decorated throughout. Jericho wore black slacks and a red, snug button-down, short-sleeved shirt. His muscles bulged out of it as it appeared to be a couple sizes too small.

"Wow," Sarah said. "You don't look bad when you wear regular people's clothes."

Jericho laughed. "What's wrong with my fatigues? They're comfortable."

"Everything and every day can't be about war, can it?"

"I don't know. I think it's the only life I've known for about fifteen years."

Sarah's forehead crumpled. "You're still in the military?"

"Oh, no." Jericho waved his hand. "What I mean is, I'm a

military contractor, and it's like my work never ends."

"Ok." Sarah nodded. "I was nervous for a second there. So how is it to finally meet your mother?"

"It's weird." Jericho rubbed his chin. "I didn't know if she was alive or dead. I just knew she'd disappeared right after I was born. I think my uncle Pat was a little dishonest with us all."

"Are you upset about that?"

"Not really." Jericho fiddled with his silver fork. "Once I came to terms with who I really was, I understood that this life can be difficult, and this is part of it."

"I don't follow," Sarah said.

"My job makes it difficult to have those types of relationships."

"Well, are you gonna be alone forever?"

Jericho knew where the conversation was headed. He saw the spark in Sarah's eyes as soon as she entered the room at the hotel. He thought Sarah was attractive, but the idea of settling down had never dawned on him. He enjoyed one-night stands and escort service because he never wanted to get attached. He believed his work would put his loved ones in danger.

The couple talked and laughed all night. Jericho enjoyed Sarah's company. It finally gave him a chance to see that his sense of humor wasn't designed to make others mad. Sarah seemed to really like listening to his jokes. She grabbed his hands several times, and she stared him in his eyes. He appreciated the eye contact and the sincerity of her laughter. *Maybe I should do stand-*

up comedy because I'm killing it tonight.

As midnight approached, Jericho and Sarah got up and prepared to leave. It was closing time, and they were the last patrons in the restaurant. A slow and light-hearted song played on the jukebox.

"I don't suppose you like to dance?" She asked.

"You know what?" Jericho grabbed her hand. "I don't do it much, but I'm in an accommodating mood tonight."

They strolled to the center of the restaurant, where there was a small space available for dancing. Jericho pulled Sarah close, and they began to slow-dance.

"This has been a nice evening," Sarah said as he leaned in closer and rested her face on Jericho's chest. "I haven't been this comfortable with someone since my husband passed."

"If you don't mind me asking, what was he like?"

"He was the strong silent type. Like you."

Jericho giggled. "Strong, yes. I don't know about the silent part, though. Most people, who know me, would say I talk *too* much."

"Really? I'd love to get to know that side of Jericho Caine too."

"Maybe, you will."

New York

Tom jogged down the empty alleyway until he got closer to the streetlight at the end. A white van sat underneath the streetlight, and Tom tip-toed toward the unmarked vehicle. He didn't see anyone in the front seat and wondered where the driver was. That was until he saw a white cloud of smoke coming from behind the van. He lay flat on the ground and looked underneath. He saw two pairs of shoes. *There are guests of honor. Only two. Looks like I won't need to be subtle about this after all.*

Tom walked up to the front of the van and quietly climbed on top of it. He crawled toward the back. He looked down and saw a tall brunette man, wearing a black leather jacket, and smoking a hand-rolled cigarette. The other man was older and shorter, with gray hair and wore a brown suit. A wooden crate sat on the ground in the middle of the men.

"It's not nice to sneak up the people," The smoking man said with a thick accent. "In fact, it's kind of rude."

Both men looked up and saw Tom looking down at them. Tom jumped down to the side of the van near the back.

"You must be Olaf Sader?" Tom clapped once and then turned to the shorter man. "And who are you, the buyer?"

"Y-You're T-T-Tom Padilla." The short man backed away. "You can't be here right now."

"On the contrary, doctor." Olaf flicked his cigarette to the side. "Let's get this over with, right now."

Olaf quickly drew his gun from his holster and fired. Tom dove to the ground and continued to roll on his side as Olaf continued to fire. Tom moved until he hit the side of a building on the other side of the alley. He popped back to his feet and pulled out his pole. It expanded until it was the length of his body. Both ends of the bar were sharpened knives. He launched it at Olaf, who dove to the ground. Before Olaf could recover, Tom ran up to him and kicked him in the face. Olaf lay flat on his back on the ground. He was conscious, but his eyes rolled back as he held his head.

Tom looked around and noticed that the shorter man had gotten away along with the wooden crate. Tom ran to the end of the alley and looked around the corner. The man walked fast but couldn't run while carrying the crate. Tom sprinted toward the man and heard a growl. He looked around, and two feet kicked him in the side of his head. He fell to the ground. Looking up, he saw a large man walking toward him. The man kicked Tom in the stomach.

"Oof." Tom grabbed his gut. "A dirty cheap shot."

"Stand up, Priest." The huge man reached down to pick up Tom by the shirt collars. "I was just introducing myself. But trust me, I don't need to cheap shot the likes of you."

"How's about me then?" Alexander appeared a few feet away. "Didn't think we'd meet again, did you, *Thaden*?"

"Wizard." Thaden flung Tom up against the wall. "Things will be different this time, for several reasons."

"How so?" Alexander asked.

Thaden turned to the side. "Boys."

Two vampires stepped out of the shadows. One was black, tall, bald, and muscular. He wore a snug black suit, which highlighted his muscular frame. The other vampire was Latino, with short slicked-back hair and also wore a black suit.

"Need help, I see," Tom said.

Thaden chuckled. "Nope, just a distraction."

Allentown Central Park

A cool breeze blew off the pond in the center of the park, where a few people were walking around. Homeless people set up tents under trees. Jericho and Sarah held hands as they slowly walked around the pond on the nearby sidewalk.

"I hate to sound pushy," Sarah said. "But, where is this thing between us headed?"

"It's not pushy at all, Sarah. I'm just not that used to being in a relationship."

"Plenty of one-night stands?"

"Not exactly. But I'm not the guy you take home to your parents."

Sarah squeezed Jericho's hand tighter. "Well, unfortunately, my parents are dead. So, that won't be a problem."

"You have the perfect answer to everything I say, don't you?" Jericho stopped and faced Sarah. "Almost as if we were meant to be."

"I don't see anything holding us back."

Jericho bent over to kiss Sarah. They stood in the center of the sidewalk and kissed for a few minutes. Jericho finally pulled away and stared into Sarah's blue eyes. *Wow! She seems like the perfect woman. Not a bad kisser either. Is this too good to be true? Wilma showing up out of nowhere, and Sarah just happen to be with her. Screw it. Why question why?*

"Do you wanna head back to my room?" Sarah asked.

"You share a room with Wilma, right?"

"I got another room for tonight." Sarah's face turned red. "Just in case."

"Great! I thought you'd never ask."

Jericho and Sarah walked back to the parking lot. They got into Jericho's blue pickup truck and pulled off.

"I wasn't going to say something earlier," Sarah began. "But didn't you have a red truck yesterday?"

Jericho smiled slyly. "I did. I don't like to get too comfortable with one."

"So, you just buy another one?"

"You can say that."

"That's sounds crazy, Jericho."

"About as crazy as my mother's neighbor going on a road trip with her to find her long-lost son."

Sarah laughed. "Good point."

They pulled up to the hotel. The room was on the other side of the hotel from Wilma's room. *I'll assume the room being on a different side of the hotel was by design. Sarah is very cunning. I like that.*

Jericho stood to the side as Sarah swiped the key card to unlock the door. She walked in and flipped the light switch on the wall. As soon as she turned around, Jericho grabbed her by her waist and hoisted her in the air to kiss her. He carried her like this for a few feet and gently placed her on the bed. Her face lit up as she giggled. Jericho turned and walked back toward the door. He pulled off the Do Not Disturb placard handing on the door handle, and placed it on the outside handle.

When Jericho turned back around to face Sarah, she was naked. She used her pointer finger to motion for him to come over. Jericho began to pull off his shirt as he walked back toward the bed.

"Come here, big boy." Sarah got under the covers and held up the cover for Jericho to join. "I've been looking forward to this."

Jericho sat on the edge of the bed and pulled off his shoes. Sarah sat behind him and brushed her hands along the spine on his back. She began to kiss the back of his neck. Jericho turned to face her, and they kissed. They fell to pillows. Sarah used both hands to grab Jericho's face while he pulled off his slacks. Once off, Jericho rolled his naked body on top of Sarah.

"Take me, Slayer." She said.

Wait a minute. Did she just call me slayer? I didn't tell her who I was. And I'm sure Wilma wouldn't have. Jericho's eyes squinted as he stopped kissing Sarah and stared into her face. He was just about to speak when she placed her finger over his lips and thrust her hips against his hips.

"Whatever you're about to say, can wait," she said.

Jericho succumbed to Sarah's gentle caress and began to kiss her neck again. *She's right. But this is weird, though. She was a married woman, and she doesn't seem like she knows what she's doing. Maybe, it's been a while for her. I mean, I'm not a sex god, but I'd like to think it's like riding a bike. I'll just try to enjoy this.*

The longer the lovemaking went on, the more comfortable Sarah seemed to become. Jericho's concerns vanished as he enjoyed hours of passionate sex...several times throughout the night. *She gets better every time. I can't believe she's not tired. I could learn to love this woman.*

Jericho nodded off and woke up when he felt the bed move. He yawned and reached over to drape his arm over Sarah's body. He quickly looked up when he realized she was gone. He scanned the room and realized Sarah's clothes weren't lying on the floor next to his anymore.

Sarah walked out of the bathroom. "Oh, you're awake."

"Are you going somewhere? What time is it?"

"About four o'clock in the morning." Sarah walked over and kissed Jericho on the forehead. "I'd better be getting back before Wilma wakes up."

"You're a grown woman. She'll understand. Besides, she seems like she was all for us getting together."

"I know. I want to break this to her slowly. I just don't want her to feel like I've somehow betrayed her trust."

"Ok." Jericho sighed. "Can we see each other later?"

"Of course. I had a great time last night."

Jericho rested his hands behind his head as he watched Sarah leaving the room. He wanted to stop her because he was ready for another round of sex. But he figured he'd see her again later. *I still don't know why she has to go. I barely even know Wilma. I'm sure she wouldn't have minded.*

The Alley

Tom and Alexander stood side by side as they were surrounded. Tom never relinquished his gaze at Thaden, who pulled Olaf back and resigned themselves to watch. The muscular vampire finally charged and punched Tom in the face, sending the demon hunter sprawling backward into an oversized metal dumpster. Tom stood and massaged his jaw. *Guy packs a punch. Let me show him that Caine isn't the only one capable of dispatching bloodsuckers.*

Tom charged the vampire and rammed his shoulder into the vampire's stomach. They fell to the ground and began to wrestle. The other vampire reached down and grabbed Tom's shoulder. Alexander swung his staff like a bat and cracked the vampire on top of the head. The vampire reached up and grabbed his head. He turned his attention to Alexander, and then leaped into the air toward the wizard. However, Alexander stepped to the side and plunged his staff into the vampire's back, which punched through the vampire's heart and came out of his chest. The vampire burst in ashes seconds later.

Tom was tossed against the side of the white van. He threw two punches at the muscular vampire, who shook them off and smiled. Tom looked down at his fist. *Oh yeah, I'm missing something.* He reached into his pocket: when his hands reemerged, his brass knuckles were on his fists. The vampire swung at Tom, who ducked and came back up with an uppercut. The vampire staggered backward, regained his balance, and grunted. He charged Tom again, but Tom pulled out his metal pole and jammed it into the vampire's chest.

Tom stared into the vampire's face and pulled out the pole. "All those muscles, and for what?"

Tom stepped back and watched as the vampire turned to ashes and blew away in the wind.

Thaden's werewolf fur appeared on one half of his body. "Dammit. I guess I'll have to take care of this myself."

Thaden sprinted down the street. He caught with the shorter man, Dr. Ranken, and stopped him. He lifted the crate over his head and smashed it to the ground. The golden dagger spilled out on the concrete. Thaden picked it up and held it over his head in one hand. A golden glow surrounded his body.

"I can feel it," Thaden said. "Centuries of knowledge, wisdom, and...and...POWER."

An invisible pulse knocked Dr. Ranken across the street, and he crashed into the side of an empty blue car. Thaden turned around to face Alexander, the source of the pulse. Tom also regrouped with his pole in hand and stood next to the wizard.

Tom twirled his pole behind Alexander's head and blocked two bullets. They turned around and spotted Olaf standing near the alley with both pistols out. Tom and Alexander stared at each other.

"Call it," Tom said. "The assassin or the – whatever Thaden is."

Alexander nodded towards Thaden. "That golden dagger seems like it's right up my alley."

"Ok." Tom glared at Olaf. "I'll take *him* then."

They prepared to head in the direction of their selected foes.

"Not so fast." Thaden pointed the dagger at Tom and Alexander. "I've got a better plan."

A golden beam of light erupted from the Takara Dagger. Alexander held out his staff to block the beam, but instead, when the golden beam collided with Alexander's staff, it expanded, and a golden field surrounded Tom and Alexander. The force field began to shrink, and Tom and Alexander pressed their hands against it.

Thaden picked up Dr. Ranken and flipped the unconscious scientist over his shoulder. He walked past Tom and Alexander toward Olaf.

"Let's go, Mr. Sader," Thaden said. "You've done a good job. We'll deal with them later."

Thaden held up the dagger. A ball of golden light flashed next to him and Olaf. The light grew and transformed into a portal. They stepped into it and it disappeared a few seconds later.

Tom dropped his weapon on the ground. "The field is closing

in, and we're running out of oxygen, Alexander."

"I know." Alexander dropped to one knee. "I can feel it too."

Tom continued to press against the golden field, and his arms grew tired. "Cast a spell or something, man!"

It was too late. Alexander's face turned blue, and he collapsed to the ground. Tom fell to one knee as the field continued to shrink. Once the force field weakened and disappeared, Tom fell to the ground on all four limbs and breathed heavily. His sight began to blur, even as fresh air invaded his lungs. However, it wasn't fast enough as he fell on his side to the ground. He looked up and saw what he thought was a bird landing in front of him. However, it was a woman, and she bent over to lean in closer to his face. Tom's eyelids flickered.

"Now we'll have some fun, Priest," she said as her voice fell off.

Tom finally passed out.

Part VII

The Connection

Tom lifted his head. His vision was still blurred but, slowly, was returning to normal. He looked down and noticed a thick, rusted chain wrapped around what bound him to a wooden chair. Both of his wrists were handcuffed to the chair's armrests, and his ankles were handcuffed to the legs. As his vision fully returned, he looked around the room. *This place looks kind of familiar. But it can't be. Looks like the basement from my childhood home.*

Cobwebs were spread throughout and appeared as though no one had entered the basement in years. A desk lamp was the only light and sat on a table against the far wall. The stairwell was on his right, and a new office chair was to his left. *Seems like I'll be joined soon by whoever is responsible for this.*

A brisk wind and the fluttering of wings brought forth Sariel. She wore white leather pants and a matching button-down shirt.

She had on black high-heeled shoes, and her hair was tied in a ponytail. She walked over and rolled the office chair in front of Tom. They locked eyes for a few seconds as she sat.

"You're an angel, right?" Tom began. "So, I'll assume you know who I am?"

"I do, Mr. Padilla." She crossed her legs. "But I'm not the kind of angel you think I am. In other words, BA and I were not friends."

"I see. What do you want from me?"

"I'm just going to keep you company until friends of mine come to claim you…and then kill you."

"Why don't you just do it now?"

"Right now, until my plans come to fruition, I still can't harm humans."

"How do your plans include me?"

"Before my brother, Michael decided he was on the wrong side of the Great War in Heaven, he was all in." She stared off at the ceiling. "He wanted nothing more than for you monkeys to succeed. And since angels are not allowed to interfere in human events, he decided, indirectly, to interfere another way."

"I'm not following, crazy lady."

"Shut up and listen, and you will." She sighed. "Besides the power to resurrect each other, and long-lasting life, Michael gave the Death Brothers another gift…a kind of immortality. He made it so they would be reincarnated for as long as supernatural creatures roamed the earth. You and Caine are the third set of Death

Brothers. You two will live until another pair is ready to take over. I was Michael's *protégé*, sort of like your beloved BA was to Gabriel."

Tom shook his head. "Wait. I'm going to stop you right there. What does your kidnapping and killing me, have to do with Caine and me?"

Sariel's Story
Fifteen Years ago, Allentown, Rhode Island

"Are you sure we're allowed to do this, brother?" I asked. "The first brothers died so gruesomely. It makes me wonder if it all was supposed to end with them."

"Trust me, Sariel," Michael began as we stared at the darkened house with only the porch light on. "The humans need our help. They will be overrun with vampires and werewolves if we don't intercede. Plus, other threats may come along."

"But are you sure he *is the one we should be bestowing this burden? He already has a destiny."*

"True. But this way, we make sure that the Death Brothers – jeez, I've always hated that name – but we ensure that they stand a chance to live as long as the first two…especially with whom he already is supposed to be."

We crept toward the small house in the middle of nowhere. It was evident that the owner was careful to stay hidden from the rest of the world. Traps were staged throughout the empty land surrounding the house. Being angels, we knew where the traps were and who they were for. There were wires, that when tripped, wooden stakes shot out from the surrounding trees. Fake grass-covered pits scattered throughout that had wooden stakes pointed upward. Cloves of garlic surrounded the entire house. Pure silver weaponry was spread around it. The house sat in a vast circle surrounded by trees, which were positioned ten feet away, so the sun could shine through, uninterrupted. A huge silver crucifix was mounted on top of the house. To an ignorant person, the place appeared to be a church.

We made our way to the house and looked through the basement window as a light popped on. There were no curtains, so we had a clear view inside. A muscular young man, and an older one, entered the basement room. The young man had short blonde hair and blue eyes. He reached his hand through a hole in the wall. He pulled out a blown blanket, which was wrapped around something that was the length of his arm. When he unwrapped the blanket, he exposed a sword in a brown sheath. He studied it first and waited for a reaction from the older man.

Using our angelic hearing, we listened as the older man revealed to the younger man what we'd been there to witness.

"For years, I've researched and trained would-be vampire slayers and hunters," the older man began. "But I never thought my own sister would give birth to the one true slayer. For years, I've cursed my father for passing on the Trident legacy to me. I'd almost given up hope when you turned eighteen, and nothing happened."

The young man took a step backward. "Uncle Pat, what are you saying? What's going on here?"

"Don't you see, Jericho? It's been you all along. We had to wait until your eighteenth birthday. We hoped this day would come soon after, but nothing happened. I guess you're a late bloomer."

Jericho unsheathed the sword and Energy flowed through his body, causing him to drop to his knees, but he still held the sword. The blade then morphed in appearance, becoming longer and wider. The name, Caine, glowed red at the sword's base.

"What's Caine, Uncle Pat?" Jericho asked.

"The sword takes on the name and persona *of the person who carries it." Pat put his hand on Jericho's shoulder. "It's what the C in your middle name stands for."*

Jericho leaned his head to the side. "I thought I was just Jericho C. Roberts like my father."

Pat smiled. "That's true. But you're a descendent of Victor Trident and Harold Caine. Harold was the original vampire slayer. The sword doesn't make mistakes. If it says that your name is Caine, then your name is Caine."

"Why haven't you told me this until now?"

"I'm sorry, Jericho. But I was being careful just in case I was wrong."

I turned to Michael and whispered. "I'm nervous, brother. What if we're wrong?"

"Don't be, sister," Michael said. "Just think. One of the original brothers specialized in hunting vampires. But now, we can

make the one true slayer, a Death Brother."

"And what about the other brother?"

"Doesn't matter. As long as we have the slayer, we're more than halfway there of ensuring the human race will have their protectors."

Michael pulled out a vial of red liquid. It was the blood of Stephen Dupree, the vampire hunter of the brothers, who magically infused it with a small portion of his soul. When they died, the brothers were more than willing to give Michael a small amount of their blood and souls so they could live on through others.

Michael, an archangel, had to be visible in Heaven. So, he left it to me to somehow get the slayer to drink the liquid. I had Michael's blessings, but even he had rules to follow. I knew I had to keep the mission a secret from other angels.

The next day I followed Jericho to the small town's grocery store. His smile lit up any room he walked into. He was polite. He helped an elderly lady retrieve items off the top shelves and a store clerk to clean up spilled tomato sauce. He represented all the good qualities Michael insisted humans could embody.

He finished his shopping and stopped at a local fast-food restaurant. He ate outside at the benches that had been set up in front of the restaurant. He waved and spoke to everyone that walked by.

"Wait a damn minute." Tom interrupted. "Are you talking about the same Jericho Caine that takes anything he wants, and disrespects everyone he meets, including angels?"

Sariel's smile disappeared. "Sounds like you don't know your friend as well as you think, Priest. Now, shut up and let me continue."

I was so infatuated with him that I forgot to try and slip the blood into his drink or food. Until then, I'd never seen a warrior who was so peaceful outside of battle. It made me wonder if he was indeed as tough as I'd been led to believe.

I watched Jericho train for several days. Patrick made him train with the sword until Pat felt Jericho could wield the sword in battle with ease. I followed them one night to an abandoned apartment building. It was dark, and most of the windows were boarded or broken. Pat waited in a pickup truck across the street and sent Jericho inside. Jericho had cut his hair into a buzz cut and wore black army fatigues and black boots. Surprisingly, being that the apartment had become a vampire lair, there wasn't a guard out front.

Even though I was invisible, I stood on top of the building and waited. I heard a commotion inside. I looked down at Pat. He opened the door and prepared to get out, but then thought better of it. I sprouted my wings and hovered down to the floor in which I heard the skirmish. I entered the bedroom window.

The outer room was lighted, and I cracked the door to peek inside. Dust floated throughout. I saw Jericho behead a vampire. The vampire's body and head turned to ashes before they hit the floor.

Another vampire kicked the door open and rushed past me to escape. He dove out of the window and crashed onto the concrete, which was five stories below. Jericho ran past me as well and dove out of the window. He landed on his feet in the middle of the street. I went over to the window and watched the vampire limping away. I assumed his healing ability was working but not fast enough. He pulled on his arm to snap his shoulder back into place.

Jericho unsheathed his sword and stood behind the vampire. "Excuse me. Are you going somewhere?"

The vampire turned to face Jericho. "You're pretty good for a mere hunter."

"I'm the slayer, blood-breath." Jericho quipped. "Your dusted, jackass crew from upstairs should have been evidence of that."

"The slayer?" The vampire frowned, and his deformed vampire face emerged. "There hasn't been a slayer for decades. Well, in that case, my name is Syrus, and that was my coven you've just eliminated. I think you were just lucky. You're no slayer. I think you're full of crap."

"Oh yeah." Jericho nodded. "Try me."

"Ok."

Syrus pulled out a knife and tossed his knife at Jericho, who blocked it away with his sword. The vampire pulled out another knife and jabbed it toward Jericho's face, who moved to the side and punched the vampire in the face. The vampire dropped to one knee and spit out a black substance. Jericho stuck out his hand and motioned for the vampire to attack again.

Pat opened the door and tried to warn Jericho, but it was too late as another vampire ran up and stabbed Jericho in the center of his back. Jericho dropped the Sword of Caine and fell on his side to the ground, with the knife still lodged in his back. Pat stabbed a wooden stake into the vampire's chest, and the vampire burst into ashes. Syrus recovered and punched Pat in the back of the head and knocked him unconscious.

Syrus then turned and stood over Jericho. "So much for being the slayer. If you were, you'd be healing right now, and I'd be trouble."

Jericho reached behind his back and pulled out the knife. "Oh. Do you mean like this?"

"That's impossible!" Syrus began to back away as Jericho stood. "The line of slayers was destroyed."

"Well, consider us back in business."

Syrus turned and ran. Jericho picked up his sword and tossed it toward the vampire: the blade whistled through the air and chopped off Syrus' head. The vampire burst into flames as Jericho walked over and reclaimed his sword. He then turned back around and rushed over to revive his uncle. He helped Uncle Pat into the passenger side of the pickup truck. Jericho got on the driver's side, and they pulled off.

I felt something tingling in my stomach. It was something that I've never felt before. I staggered back to the wall and moved my hands down my body. They stopped as I reached my crotch. The more I thought about Jericho, the more my body began to overheat.

Watching him in action had done something to me that was strictly forbidden within the ranks of angels. I was attracted to a human.

I knew I had to fulfill my obligation to my mentor, Michael. I sprouted my wings and took off toward the Trident home. I was about five minutes ahead of Jericho and Uncle Pat. I went into the house and looked around. I had no clue what I was going to do until an idea formed in my head. I went to the refrigerator and saw a half-full bottle of cranberry juice labeled 'Jericho.' I poured the blood inside and shook the bottle. I became invisible again as I heard the door open. Just as I thought, Jericho went into the kitchen and got the juice from the fridge. He drank the entire bottle.

"This tastes weird," he said as he tossed the empty bottle into the trash. "It must be the adrenaline still rushing through me."

I waited outside and watched Jericho through the window. He took off his shirt. His body was sweaty, and his muscles glistened off the overhead light. He looked in the dresser mirror at his back. The wound had healed. I sat on the ground, stared for a few more minutes until I heard fluttering wings. Michael landed next to me.

"I'll assume you've completed your task, sister," he said.

"I have." I stood. "I was just going to watch some more to make sure everything is going as planned."

Michael patted me on the shoulder. "There's no need. Now, we must go and find the other one. I have a few people in mind. But I'll let you have the honor of choosing the other Death Brother from that bunch."

"Wow!" My eyes opened wider. "Thank you, brother."

Two weeks later, I arrived in New York City. I'd just come from Paris and studied the second to last person of the three men that Michael had on his shortlist. I landed on top of a house in Brooklyn. I jumped to the ground and peered through the window. A Latino family stood in their living room with two priests. One of the priests was in his thirties, and the other was around twenty-two. I was there to watch Father Peter, the older of the two. He had performed at least two exorcisms throughout Europe and had settled in New York. The mother and father of the Latino family were convinced that their youngest daughter was possessed. She was in a locked bedroom upstairs.

Father Peter stood after praying with the parents in the living room. He motioned for his young apprentice to follow him up the stairs. Father Peter slowly unlocked and opened the bedroom door. The little girl, around five years old, lay in the bed. Her face was disfigured, and the room was cold. She'd used scissors to cut off her long black hair, which lay on the floor next to the bed.

"I see you haven't come alone, Father." The little girl spoke in a deep and scraggly voice. "You've also brought your winged friend for backup."

Father Peter's eyes tightened as if he didn't know what she meant. His apprentice also had a confused expression on his face. However, I knew the demon had sensed my presence.

"Wait a second." Tom interrupted again. "I remember this story. Are you trying to tell me that you originally came there that night make Father Peter the second Death Brother?"

"Yes," Sariel said. "Little did I know that the demon would jam those scissors into Father Peter's neck and kill him before he could utter one word from the exorcism. Then, the even bigger surprise was seeing his apprentice, a young priest named Father Thomas Padilla, step up and do battle with a powerful demon. Even though you let that little girl die, you vanquished the demon on your first exorcism. You thought you were a failure but – "

"I've never lived that down." Tom dropped his head. "I had to look at her parents in the face and tell them she was gone. But getting rid of the demon *was a victory?*"

"You impressed me, Thomas." Sariel folded her arms. "I then knew you were the real reason I was there. It was fate."

"But how and when did you poison me?"

"Easy." Sariel laughed. "You loved Catalina's Mexican Restaurant and their house special red wine."

Tom turned his head to the side to try to think back to that time. "You bastard." He peered back up at Sariel. "*You* did all this?"

"You're smart, Tom." Sariel leaned forward in her chair. "You were the right age, and everything you do is done so professionally…even though *you did* give up the priesthood. You were the perfect fit and counter-balance for my Jericho."

"*Your Jericho?*"

"Yes. He is mine. And you've worn out your place in his life. I was hoping the Taki girl would pull you away from Jericho. But it seems fate had other plans for her. Now you'll have to die, long before she wakes up."

"Are you saying that you…"

"Ha. Ha. Ha." Sariel threw her head back. "Michael taught me well. Human manipulation is what I'm best at, among other things."

"No! I don't believe you."

Sariel stood. "I can see you need some time to think. I'll just wait upstairs until my plan for your demise arrives."

Tom dropped his head. *Has this really been someone's plan from the start? Does free will not exist? It's what truly separates the angels from humans. They obey, but we can choose to do so or not. Is she telling me the truth, or is this some sort of trick?*

Tom closed his eyes and tried to think back to the night he met Jericho. It was ten years ago, and Tom had stumbled onto a vampire nest in Brooklyn. He had tortured a demon the night before and was told there was a more powerful demon in the area. It was getting late, and the neighborhood he arrived at was in the ghetto. He walked down a street with small houses on each side of the road, which made for more places on the block. All the streetlights were burned out except for one that flickered.

Tom spotted the house he was told about. It was the only house on the street with a tall wooden fence. It was as high as Tom's shoulders. As he got closer, he noticed two young black men with Uzis, patrolling the exterior. They both had short afros, blue jeans, and white t-shirts. Tom looked down at his watch and concluded that it took the two men ten minutes to circle the house.

Once they walked past again, he decided to sprint to the porch.

He slowly walked up the stairs. There where windows on each side of the front door, but they were painted black. *Weird. I guess they just like their privacy. I've never known demons to strictly like darkness, though.*

Tom bent down to one knee and pulled out a switchblade from an ankle holster. He stuck the knife in the keyhole and tried to unlock the door. Suddenly, he heard what sounded like metal trashcans slamming against the house. He stood up straight and turned to the side. One of the young men sailed by and landed in the front yard. Bright security lights, located along the side of the house, lit up. Tom reached inside his inner jack pocket and pulled out his brass knuckles. He put them on both hands and walked back down the porch stairs. The young man slid backward on his butt and ignored Tom. *What in the hell is going on? He doesn't even care that I'm standing here.*

Tom heard heavy footsteps approaching from the side of the house. He turned slightly to his left and saw a huge shadow getting bigger as it got closer. Tom turned his attention to it. It belonged to a tall, muscular man, about six-foot-seven inches tall. He had short blonde hair and wore black army fatigues with combat boots.

"Who are you, and what have you done with Bootsy?" The man on the ground asked.

"Bootsy?" The huge man said. "Was that his name? Well, he's what I like to call, dusted."

The man, still seated, backed up against the gate. "Jesus, man.

Y-You're him. You're him!"

"Took you long enough." The huge man reached behind his back and pulled out a sword. "I was starting to feel disrespected."

"Wait a minute." Tom stepped in between the two men. "Just who in the hell are you, and what are you planning to do with that sword?"

Jericho held up the sword in front of Tom. "The name is on the sword." He finally studied Tom from head to toe. "And you're in my way...priest."

Tom looked at the sword and saw the name Caine engrave near the sword's base. "What's a Caine?"

"It's Jericho Caine," Jericho said. "I'm the vampire slayer. Now, step aside. I have work to finish here."

Three black men walked out the front door, with the middle one clapping. He was muscular, a little smaller than Jericho. The other two were armed with Uzis. They all had on blue jeans, white t-shirts, just like the guards. Jericho and Tom turned to face them. The man in the middle stepped back and pushed the two men at his side to the front.

"I'm honored," the leader said. "Looks like the info I got was correct. And here I thought we'd go on for years without landing on the radar of the new slayer."

Jericho took a step closer. "Finally, the leader of this boy band decides to join us. You know, you could have flown under the radar for years, Tobias, until you started killing children and even turning some."

"What can I say?" Tobias began. "We're hungry and needed to replenish our ranks. So, is the priest your new *protégé*? Explains why they want him dead too."

"I don't need a pro – "

"I'm nobody's *protégé*." Tom cut in. "And what are you guys trying to say? You're vampires? And who are the '*they*' you speak of?"

Jericho turned to Tom. "You're not too quick, are you, Priest?"

Before Jericho could turn back toward Tobias, he was punched in the face. He wiped the side of his lip with his hand. There was no blood. He spat anyway, and then he stared at Tobias' henchman, the one who punched him. The henchman turned back to Tobias with a confused expression on his face.

"What are you looking at me for?" Tobias asked. "Kill them both."

The vampire that lay on the ground grabbed Tom from behind in a chokehold. The other henchmen attacked Jericho, who punched the vampire in the throat and sent him sprawling to the ground clutching its neck.

"I don't have time to give you a crash course on how to kill vampires, Priest." Jericho turned back to Tom. "But I can at least make it a fair fight."

Jericho punched the vampire that was choking Tom in the face. He fell to the ground, and Tom bent over to regain his breath. Jericho turned back to the house as the other henchman attempted to escape behind Tobias. Jericho launched his sword at the vampire in the rear and punctured his back, bursting through his chest. The vampire burst into fiery ashes. Jericho walked up the stairs to retrieve his sword, but the vampire that Jericho chopped in the throat grabbed Jericho's shoulder. Jericho grabbed the vampire's wrist and twisted it, snapping his arm in four places. The vampire dropped to his knees, holding his arm while Jericho reached inside his oversized pants pocket and pulled out a wooden stake. He jammed the stake into the vampire's heart, and he turned ashes a second later.

Jericho turned around to watch the commotion behind him. He stepped back and sat on the porch stairs. The vampire and Tom wrestled on the ground with the vampire on top. He leaned in closer, attempting to bite Tom in the neck. *Should I help this wimpy-looking priest? I mean, he did show up and just jump in my business. I'll just see how this plays out.*

Tom struggled to reach in his pockets and pulled out a small glass vial of yellow liquid. He shoved the bottle in the vampire's open mouth. The glass didn't break, so Tom punched the vampire in the jaw. The vampire stood and staggered backward. He began to cough and spit out pieces of broken glass.

"W-What in the hell are you trying to do to me?" The vampire managed to ask.

"Wait a second." Jericho stood. "You're Father John Padilla's kid?"

"I'm no kid." Tom got back to his feet and brushed off his

pants. "But yes, John is my father."

The vampire coughed again. "Who the hell cares, man? What are you trying to do with that pee-looking stuff?"

With a quick stroke from his sword, Jericho cut off the vampire's head. Before his head or body hit the ground, they burst into a fiery cloud of ashes.

"Sorry about the delay," Jericho said as he walked toward Tom. "I've read all about your father. That's his Detox that you just rammed down that suckhead's throat." He burst into laughter. "Sorry, padre, but I think that stuff only works on demons."

Tom finally let a smile creep on his face. "Yeah, I see that now. I've never encountered a vampire before. But I heard they were half-demons, so I figured I'd give it a shot. And it's *my* Detox now."

"What's a demon hunter doing at a vampire lair?" Jericho asked.

"I was told that a demon I've been hunting was held up here."

"By whom?"

"Another demon."

"So, a demon lied to a demon hunter about the where-a-bouts of another demon? That can't be something new, Priest."

"Well, I had a crucifix pressed to his head while threatening to pour Detox down its throat. So, I figured I'd believe him. Apparently, getting me here was his plan, probably to have these vampires kill me."

"Hmm," Jericho rubbed the stubble on his chin. "Vampires

and demon's working together. They don't exactly play well with each other. What gives?"

"Tobias said they were expecting me to show up. I'll assume somebody wanted us both here."

"Dammit!" Jericho snapped his fingers. "Tobias."

Jericho turned and ran toward the house, and Tom followed. They ran through the house toward the back. Jericho ran into a den in the far corner of the house. Tobias stepped out from behind the door and kick Jericho in the back as he ran past. Jericho fell forward and tripped over a rug. He crashed into a big brown desk, but he caught himself before tumbling to the floor. However, Tobias closed the door and locked it from the outside.

Tom stopped running a few feet in front of Tobias, who smiled and exposed his fangs. He pounded his fist in his other hand and began to slowly walk toward Tom.

"It's funny," Tobias said as saliva dripped from his mouth. "In certain circles, killing a priest is forbidden. But I was told to kick the hell out of you, turn you, and then let *you* feast on the slayer."

Tom's eyes tightened. "Told by whom?"

"Doesn't matter. Just know that I'm going to enjoy this."

My God. It was all some master plan and a test. My first encounter with Jericho was a damn test. Dusting Tobias was one of the proudest moments in my young life. I thought I'd proven myself to Caine. Turns out, I was just proving myself to the angels.

Allen Town, Rhode Island

Jericho couldn't sleep. It was obvious to him that Sarah was out of practice, but the sex had gotten better later on. He wanted to see her again, so he got up and put on his clothes. He went down to the lobby and got three cups of coffee and placed them in a cup holder. He went up to Wilma's and Sarah's room and knocked.

Wilma opened the door, still in her white bathrobe. She wiped her eyes and smiled at her massive son as he stood at the door with a big smile on his face.

"Wow. Someone had a good night," she said.

"It was great!" Jericho replied. "I just brought you, ladies, some coffee and wanted to know if you wanted to go out for breakfast."

"I could eat." Wilma grinned. "How's about you go back to get Sarah, and meet me back here in about thirty minutes."

"Sarah's not here? She should have been back hours ago."

Wilma turned back to survey the room. "No. She hasn't been here since you picked up her last night."

"Hmm," Jericho mused. "She told me she was coming back here. Where could she be?"

"I didn't want to say this earlier." Wilma sat on the edge of the bed. "There have been some strange things going on with her from the beginning."

"Really?" Jericho entered the room and leaned up against the door after he closed it. "Like what?"

Wilma stared at the wall. "Like appearing out of nowhere when we first met at the grocery store. Her getting close to me even though there's a huge age difference."

"That's not really so shocking, Wilma. She *is* a widow."

"Other things too. Like how she got into our old house and finding the box that led to – oh my God. To you."

"Me?" Jericho asked with a confused expression on his face. "Why me?"

"Every conversation she and I had recently always ended with me talking about my son. Her insisting on coming on this trip, and now you two finally getting together."

"That's not too farfetched. But now, it depends on your response to my next question."

"What is it, son?"

Jericho bent to one knee in front of Wilma. "Did you tell her I was the slayer?"

Wilma shook her head rapidly. "Of course not. I'm a Trident at the end of the day. I know the importance of keeping that a secret."

Jericho stood again. He stared at Wilma and then on the floor. He knew his mother was telling the truth. He'd let his emotions and sexual desires get in the way of realizing the truth. Sarah had called him the slayer when they made love. *Dammit! I knew I should have questioned it right then. But technically, she hasn't done anything wrong...so far. The question is, who is she, and what does she want?*

127

Basement in New York

Tears welled up in Tom's eyes as he heard footsteps coming down the stairs. He blinked quickly to get rid of the tears. He waited for the door to open. When it did, Sariel, Thaden, Dr. Ranken, and Olaf marched in.

"He's all yours." Sariel held out her hand toward Tom. "I hope your revenge is sweet, cold, and slow, doctor."

"Revenge?" Tom stared at Ranken. "Am I supposed to know what this is about?"

"You will, demon hunter." Dr. Ranken clapped once and rubbed his hands together. "You will."

Thaden turned to Sariel. "What did you do with the wizard?"

"I left him passed out on the street," Sariel replied. "He is of no consequence to us."

Thaden grunted. "You're not worried that he won't try to find this one? And what about Caine?"

Sariel walked toward the stairs and stopped. "Don't worry about Caine. He's distracted for now."

Sariel walked up the stairs and left. Thaden backhanded Tom and knocked saliva from his mouth. Tom's head rocked to the side.

Tom shook of the strike. "That's all you got?"

Thaden cocked his hand to swing again

"No!" Dr. Ranken stepped in front of Thaden. "Let me."

Dr. Ranken pulled off his sports jack and rolled up his sleeves. He punched Tom several times in the face. Tom's head jarred back a few times, and his eyes rolled backward. Each time he returned to his original position, he had a smile on his face, even though he bled from his mouth and nose.

"You must only be the brains of the operation." Tom licked the blood from the corner of his mouth. "Because my mom throws a better punch than that."

Thaden and Olaf erupted in a burst of laughter that caused Dr. Ranken to shoot them a look of disgust.

"Ok, Priest," Dr. Ranken said. "You asked for this."

"Wait!" Thaden held up his hand. "Do you hear that?"

Dr. Ranken looked around the room, "What?"

"Sorry, Lord Thaden, sir." Olaf cut in. "But I don't hear anything either."

Tom smiled.

Thaden walked closer to Tom. "I hear a distinct beeping sound."

Dr. Ranken glared at Olaf and then Thaden with a confused expression on his face. "Not everyone has a vampire or werewolf's hearing."

Thaden bent down to one knee as Olaf moved in closer as well. Thaden reached inside Tom's pocket and pulled out a set of brass knuckles, which he tossed over his shoulders. He reached in the pocket again and found a small metallic object. A tiny red light flashed from the object.

"I think it's a tracking device." Thaden balled his fist and crushed it. "Did the angel know about this? Did no one search this guy?"

Suddenly, there was a loud pop. Thaden jumped back to his feet and stepped away. A flashing portal opened in the middle of Tom and Olaf. A hand reached out of the portal and grabbed Olaf's shoulder and pulled the assassin inside it. Then, Alexander stepped out with his staff in hand.

Dr. Ranken slid behind Thaden. "It's the wizard!"

Thaden reached behind his back, and the Takara Dagger appeared in his hand. "Do you want some more, wizard? I'll give it to you."

"I didn't come here to fight you." Alexander held out his staff and put his hand on Tom's shoulder. "I've come for this. Ianuae Magicae (teleport)."

A white glow engulfed Tom and Alexander, and they began to shrink. Once it was the size of a baseball, the glow shot through the air and into the portal. A scuffle erupted from inside the portal, and the sound of fists meeting flesh rang out. Thaden slowly approached it. However, he stopped as Olaf was tossed out of the flashing doorway and landed at Thaden's feet. The portal closed immediately after.

Allentown Rhode Island

Jericho had left, and Wilma continued to get dressed. She put on makeup and slipped on her blue dress. As she bent over on the bed to tighten the strap on her sandals, she couldn't help but smile. Aside from the mystery surrounding Sarah, everything was going as she hoped. She'd gotten the closure she wanted by going home. *Yes, finding out Patrick was dead hurts, but knowing that my son Jericho is alive makes up for it.*

The progress she had made with Jericho was the reason she was thrilled. His last words replayed in her head.

"I want to get to know you better, Wilma," He'd said. "I want to get to the point where I can call you 'mom.' That's where I want our relationship to go."

"We will get there." Wilma had replied. "Take your time. When it feels right, I want to feel like I should have thirty-five years ago when you were born."

Wilma already felt that way, though. It was just a matter of Jericho getting to the point where she was already. Wilma stood and pulled down her dress. She walked over to the nightstand and picked up her purse. As she put the straps over her shoulder, she glared at the untouched empty bed that was Sarah's. She walked toward the door and opened it.

Sarah stepped out in front of the door. "Wilma, are you ready to go eat?"

"I'm not sure I should be going anywhere with you, Sarah…if that is your name."

"What are you talking about, Miss Wilma? Why would you say that?"

Wilma stepped back into the room. "Jericho and I are questioning what your true intentions are. You haven't been honest with me, young lady."

"I'm Sarah. You've known me for months."

"I thought I did."

Sarah looked both ways down the hall and then stepped inside the room. "I'll tell you what. I have a business in New York. Ride with me, and I'll explain everything on the way."

"No!" Wilma exclaimed. "You tell me now." Wilma turned and walked back to place her purse on the bed. "Or I'm not going anywhere with you."

"I'm sorry you feel that way."

Wilma spun around and was hit with a metal object. She fell on the bed, bounced off it and onto the floor. Her eyes rolled back, and she was out.

Part VIII

The Show Is Over

New York

Wilma's eyes flickered as they opened. She tried to focus, but it was dark. She noticed a light on the floor that appeared from what she assumed was a door. She tried to move and realized she was on a twin-sized bed. Her wrists and ankles were bound with rope. As her eyesight settled, she looked around and saw a hint of light from the window. She then knew it was dark out as she saw a few stars in the sky from the diagonal slit in the middle of the curtain.

"Help!" She screamed. "Somebody help!"

She heard footsteps coming closer and saw shadows from the light under the door. The door opened, and a tall shadowy figure stood in the doorway.

"Ah. You're awake," A woman's voice said. "I thought I was going to have to come in and wake you. Because I do want you awake for what comes next."

"Who are you? What do you want with me?" Wilma asked.

"My name is Sariel." She walked closer to the bed. "You knew me as Sarah, but now, the show is over."

Wilma closed her eyes to think. "Sarah. I remember now. I trusted you."

"Yes, you did, until you didn't. But don't worry. I won't need anything else from you, except your body."

The ceiling light clicked on in the center of the room, exposing the tall angel Sariel. She stepped to the side and gestured toward the door, where a Latino young boy appeared and stepped into the doorway. He was around twelve years old. His eyes were glowing red, and he had long black hair with uncanny scars on his cheeks and forehead. Saliva dripped from the corners of his mouth.

Wilma glared up at Sariel. "What's going on? Why is he here? And what's wrong with his face?"

"I wouldn't be worried about that, Miss Wilma." Sariel rubbed her hands together. "But then again, in a few minutes, you won't care anymore."

Wilma looked at the young man again. "What are you about to do?"

"You'll see," Sariel said as she looked down at the young man. "Make it quick. We have work to do."

The young man walked over to the bed and sat on the edge. Wilma squirmed, but she couldn't move. The young man leaned over and grabbed both sides of Wilma's face so that they were eye to eye. He squeezed Wilma's jaw to force her mouth open. The young man's red eyes rolled back, and his head fell back as well. He began to shake, and his mouth opened. He growled. He grunted. Finally, he began to cough, and a yellow smoke left his mouth and entered into Wilma's mouth. The young man's body fell to the floor in front of Sariel, who let out a smile of approval.

Wilma's eyes opened again. This time, they were red. She let out a deep and sinister chuckle. She looked down at her hands and snapped the rope that held her wrists together. She did the same with the rope around her ankles.

"Are you ready, Lord Brodus?" Sariel asked. "It is time to fulfill your debt."

"I am ready." Brodus' deep and scratchy voice echoed throughout the room. "Does anyone know we are working together? Angels and demon are not supposed to form alliances."

"No one knows…yet." Sariel interlocked her hands behind her back. "But I will help you get revenge on the priest. In turn, it will help me gain favor with the slayer, after this debacle with his mother."

"Finally, Tom Padilla will pay for destroying my master, Desoto." The demon stood. "It wasn't easy to take over a clan of demons when your former leader was more powerful and ancient. But how will this ploy gain you favor with the slayer?"

"When you kill Padilla," Sariel began. "I will come along and pretend to cast you out of Wilma soon after. I forgot to mention. The body you're possessing belongs to the slayer's mother."

"And who said angels weren't devious?" Brodus' sinister

laughed returned. "I like this plan. Let's get started."

About an hour passed when a white van pulled up to the gigantic church on the corner. Wilma was pushed out of the side sliding door and onto the street. The van peeled off. Two nuns, who were standing on the front steps talking, ran over and tend to Wilma. Her knees and elbows were bruised from the tumble. The nuns helped her to her feet.

"Are you ok, ma'am?" The short older nun asked.

"I-I think I am," Wilma said as she stood and brushed off her dress. "Where am I?"

"You are at the newly renamed Saint John's Catholic Church." The other black and younger nun responded.

"Renamed?" Wilma asked.

"Yes," the young woman said. "Renamed after Father John Padilla. He just recently received sainthood status."

Wilma grunted. "Is that a fact?"

The nuns put an arm around Wilma's waste and helped her walked toward the church. They stepped onto the sidewalk, and an alarm blared. They all covered their ears to block out the sound."

"My Lord, what is that?" the older nun asked.

Wilma smiled. "I think it's the demon alarm."

"Demon?" Both nuns looked at Wilma.

"Yes," Wilma said. "Me."

Wilma's face turned pale, and Brodus' scars appeared on her forehead and cheeks. She grabbed the nun's necks from the back and slammed their heads together. They fell to the ground. The older white nun was unconscious. The young black nun grabbed both sides of her head and stared up at Brodus.

"Too bad." Brodus raised his foot. "You should have at least pretended to pass out."

Brodus brought his foot down and stomped the young nun in the head. Her head and face exploded in a puddle of flesh, bone, and blood. She died instantly. Brodus dragged its feet across the concrete to wipe off the bloody stains on his shoes.

He looked up and smiled at the crucifix atop the church. He then walked toward the steps of the church and sat as the alarm continued blare in the background. He bit his nails as he took a step up the stairs. He tried to walk up to another step, but he bounced back as he ran into an invisible force field. He tried again and again, but he could not proceed forward. One of the church doors opened. A priest and three more nuns exited the building. The priest grabbed his crucifix that hung from his neck.

"Go back to hell, demon." The priest demanded. "You cannot enter here,"

"Are you doing this, Priest?" Brodus asked. "I have the ability to enter any place of worship. If you are doing this, let's see if this barrier also protects you from my power."

Brodus' eyes glowed red as he raised his hands. The priest began to float up into the air. He rose to the top of the church. Brodus quickly lowered his arms, and the priest fell to the ground, breaking his neck. His eyes remained open as they looked up at the nuns, who screamed and ran back into the church. They slammed the door behind them. Brodus attempted to follow but was again stopped by the force field.

"This is impossible," Brodus said. "Nothing can stop me…unless. Wow! This place has been blessed by an angel. I should have known. It's Padilla's church."

Police sirens sounded out as the sun began to rise. Brodus turned around to face the oncoming police cars. He raised his hands and debris raised up from the ground. Newspaper dispensers, light poles, garbage cans, and stones floated into the air and crashed into the police car windshields. The cars swerved out of the way, crashing into parked vehicles and businesses on the street. One officer got out of the passenger side of the vehicle and fired his pistol. The bullet bounced off Brodus' head, who turned in the direction of the cop and raised his hands. A small red car was hurled at the police officer. Just as it was about to hit the cop, who managed to duck, the car was cut in half and fell to the side.

Brodus had a shocked expression on his face as the dust cleared from the trashed car. Jericho placed his sword back in the sheath on his back.

"Wasn't expecting that, were you?" Jericho asked as he walked toward the church. "Wait a sec. Wilma? What the hell is going on?"

"Slayer," said Brodus while cocking his head to the side. "You're not the Death Brother I was expecting."

"Well, I'm the one you've got, demon." Jericho put his hands on his hips. "Now, how, and why, are you in Wilma's body?"

"What's wrong, Slayer?" Brodus threw his head back and laughed. "You don't like my new digs? Besides, I was told you'd be busy with other things."

"Told. By whom?" Jericho asked. "Who are you working for?"

"I work for no one, muscle-head." Brodus took a step down one of the stairs. "But just so you don't get any ideas, your mother is still alive in here with me. Makes me untouchable."

We'll see about that. Jericho turned, walked down the middle of the street, and jumped in front of an oncoming black, town car. He walked around to the driver's side, snatched the door off, and threw it on the sidewalk.

"Phone?" Jericho held out his hand to the older driver, who was dressed in a black suit. "Come on. I don't have all day."

The man handed Jericho his cell phone. He glanced at the door on the sidewalk and shook his head. Jericho pointed down the street, and the man pressed down hard on the gas, and the car screeched as it pulled off. Jericho called Tom's apartment phone, but the latter hadn't answered his pages all morning.

"Come on, Priest. Pick up."

Jericho shook his head when the answering machine picked up. After he left a message, he looked back toward the church and saw Brodus waiting on the church steps. Jericho let out a deep sigh. *I can see that this is gonna be a long day.* He walked back toward the church.

Tom and Alexander

The bright light dissipated, and Tom and Alexander swelled back to normal size. Tom looked around and realized Alexander had teleported them back to Tom's apartment.

"Liberatio (release)." Alexander pointed his staff at Tom, who was still confined to the chair.

Tom massaged his wrists as the restraints disappeared and he stood. "Seems like that took longer than before, Alexander. Did we take the scenic route?"

"Sorry about that, Tom," Alexander said. "But the teleportation spell was put together on the fly. Plus, with you being handcuffed to a chair, it made things a little trickier…and longer."

"That's ok. We got away, and that's all that matters."

Tom placed his hands on his hips and scanned his apartment. *This place never looked so good.* He glanced over to his in-table and saw a red light blinking rapidly. It was from his older model answering machine. He then reached in his front pants pocket and realized this pager was missing. *I didn't even notice it was gone before. But that message had better be from Jericho, dammit.* He walked over and pressed the button on the machine.

"Mr. Padilla. This is Dr. Walker from the hospital. She's awake."

Tom was frozen for a second. He looked up at Alexander and then back at the machine. Tom pressed the rewind button. He pushed the play button again. He wanted to make sure he'd heard the message correctly.

"Mr. Padilla. This is Dr. Walker from the hospital. She's awake."

The messaged was about two hours old. Tom quickly headed for the front door.

"Aren't you gonna listen to the rest of the messages?" Alexander asked.

Tom stopped walking. "No. I've heard all I need to hear."

"What if Caine tried to reach you?" Alexander pleaded. "You said you'd lost contact with him."

"Screw him!" Tom exclaimed. "This is more important. I'd been trying to reach him all night, for crying out loud."

"Well, I'm gonna listen." Alexander walked over and pressed the button on the answering machine. "We need help. Things are getting crazy."

"Dammit, Priest. I've been paging you all morning. There's a situation at your old church. How have you not gotten an alert? Call me back...ASAP!"

Alexander folded his arms as he stared at Tom. "He sounds stressed."

"So," Tom said dryly.

"I've haven't known Caine nearly as long as you. But I've never heard him sound like that."

Tom put his hands on his hips and dropped his head. He knew Alexander was right. Jericho wasn't the type to worry. *And knowing Jericho as I do, that actually sounded like fear.*

Alexander's eyebrows raised. "Well?"

"Fine." Tom sighed. "You go to the hospital. And I'll go to the church. How's about a lift?"

"Are you sure you won't need me at the church?

"I'm not sure. But I would prefer Susie had someone she knows at the hospital. She's gotta be confused right now."

"I agree." Alexander held out his staff. "Aperta portal (open portal)."

A bright light flashed, and a portal opened next to Tom. He nodded at Alexander and stepped into the luminous void.

Saint John's Catholic Church

Brodus stood and cracked his neck as Jericho approached. "I thought you'd runoff. I was saving this ass-whooping for the priest. But you'll just have to do for now."

One of the double church doors swung open from behind the demon, and Tom stepped out. "If it's my medicine to take, I'll take it."

Brodus spun around. "Padilla. My luck just keeps getting better."

Jericho moved closer and nodded at Tom. Brodus looked at Jericho and then back to Tom. He leaped into the air and dove on Tom, knocking them both back into the church.

"Thanks for the ride across the barrier," Brodus said as he and Tom scrambled around on the floor. "When I'm done with you, I'm going to burn this place to the ground."

Jericho rushed up the stairs and kicked open the door. He saw Tom and Brodus wrestling around on the floor in the center aisle of the church. Brodus rolled on top and stood. He stomped on Tom's chest and ran toward the pulpit. Jericho ran after him, but Brodus turned and lifted his arms. The front pew shook as it rose off the ground. Brodus thrust his arms toward Jericho: the pew was launched at the slayer. Jericho ducked, and the pew landed behind him. Brodus jumped up to the pulpit and picked up the thick oversized bible. He threw it at Jericho and bounced the giant book off the top of the slayer's head. Jericho dropped to one knee. Before he could stand again, the wooden microphone stand crashed into his back, knocking him face-first to the floor.

Brodus erupted in laughter. He looked beyond Jericho's body for Tom, but he was gone. Brodus turned to the right and was cracked in the forehead by a brass-knuckled fist. His head began to smoke as the crucifix emblem from Tom's brass knuckles was imprinted on the demon's head. Brodus fell backward to the floor of the pulpit, and his eyes rolled back. Tom jumped up and came down with his knees on Brodus' chest. Tom cocked his fist back and prepared to punch the demon again.

"T-Tom, no!" Jericho held out his hand. "That's my...my mother."

Tom stared at Jericho and then back at Brodus. "What? What are you talking about, Caine?"

Jericho got to his feet and staggered toward the pulpit. "This is Wilma Trident. My mother."

Tom's eye's tightened. "Holy cr – "

Brodus threw his arms forward and a powerful wind blew Tom across the church, who crashed into the farthest wall and fell into a sitting position. Brodus tried to sit up, but he was smashed in the face with the huge bible that he'd thrown at Jericho. The back of Brodus' head smacked the floor, and he passed out.

Jericho walked over and helped Tom to his feet, who managed to bend over and rest his hands on his knees. He breathed heavily and then stared up at Jericho.

"Are you kidding me, Caine?" Tom asked. "I didn't even know your mother was alive. Or that you even had one. I thought you just appeared one day as the slayer."

"Ha. Ha. Hilarious, smart guy. But we need to restrain it, and you need to do your thing."

"And what's that?"

"Exorcise his ass."

"Tom shook his head. "Language, Caine. This is still a church. But let's just kill the thing. We don't have time for this."

"Wilma is still alive in there, Thomas. Or I would have chopped off its head long ago."

"Yeah." Tom nodded. "I was wondering why you hadn't done that yet."

New York Memorial Hospital

Alexander slowly opened the door and walked into the room. He took off his baseball hat and inched closer to the bed. The young Japanese woman appeared to sleep, so Alexander sat in the nearby green leather recliner. He clasped his hands together and lowered his head.

"Alexander?" A faint voice said.

Alexander looked up. "Susie? Thank Merlin, you're awake."

"What happened?" Susie asked.

"I'll fill you in. But how long have you been conscious?

"Just a few hours…I think."

"What's the last thing you remember?"

Susie closed her eyes, opened them again, and stared at the ceiling. "I remember fighting my aunt Ahmya. She was trying to kill – oh my God, Tom. Is Tom, ok?"

"Yes." Alexander grabbed Susie's hand. "You saved him and yourself. We won. But Tom is handling another emergency right now. I'm sure it's important too because you waking up is all that he's thought about since…well since you've been out."

Susie sighed. "What about Caine, BA?"

"The slayer is ok." Alexander took a deep breath. "BA didn't make it."

"The angel's d-dead?"

"Yes. Killed by the Hangman. That's a long story. But I'm guessing we have time."

Saint John's Church

Jericho sat at the desk in what used to be Tom's office in the back of the church. He occasionally looked over to watch Wilma's unconscious body. She was strapped to a cot at the waist with rope. The cot sat across the room against the far wall. *She doesn't look well. This is all my fault. She's involved in this because of me. I can't let that demon have her.*

Wilma's eyes opened. "Son? What's going on?"

Jericho stood and crept over to the cot. "Wilma? Is that you?"

"It is, my son. Now cut me loose, and let's get out of this church. I don't feel comfortable here."

Jericho cocked his head to the side. "Um. How do you know where we are…*demon*?"

Wilma's face turned pale, and Brodus' scars appeared on her face again. "It doesn't matter whom you talk to, Slayer." Wilma's voice slowly transformed into Brodus' menacing voice. "Me or this slut. Neither of you will leave this dump alive."

"You, demon slime," Jericho reached back and pulled his sword from the sheath. "Let her go. She has nothing to do with this."

"That's right," Tom entered the room with a bible in hand. "This is between you and us, demon."

Brodus laughed. "Ah-ha. The demon slayer. Just the person I've been waiting for."

Brodus closed his eyes and struggled to get free. He opened

146

his eyes with a confused expression on his face.

"What have you done to me?"

"What's wrong, demon?" Tom smiled. "Can't use your powers? Do you feel that burning sensation running down your back? It's because you're lying on my cross."

"You son of a whore, Priest," Brodus squirmed. "Do you really think I need my powers to defeat you? You don't remember me, do you?"

"Should I?" Tom replied.

"I was there when you killed my master, Desoto." Brodus glanced at Jericho. "Now, I will take my revenge out on you and that 'death brother' of yours."

"Jericho," Tom turned his back to the demon to face Jericho and whispered. "You may want to step out for this. Trust me, this isn't your mother anymore. It may get – well, it may get rough."

"We're in this together," Jericho said. "I won't get in the way."

"Suit yourself."

Brodus laughed. "Yes, Thomas. Let him stay. I promise it will be fun."

Tom put on this priest's collar. He pulled out a silver vial of holy water and rinsed his hands. Then, he turned to a page in his bible and stood next to the cot. As he was about to speak, Brodus spat in Tom's face. Tom wiped away the spit as Brodus laughed.

Tom turned his head to the side. "Jericho, you need to leave."

"Why?" Jericho asked.

Brodus spoke in Wilma's voice. "Because he wants to beat me. He wants to hurt me. Please don't let him, son. Please."

"Don't listen to it, Caine." Tom pleaded as he bent over and put his hand over Brodus' mouth. "He will try to turn us against each other."

Brodus bit Tom's hand. The priest pulled his hand back and balled his fist.

"See," Brodus said in Wilma's voice again. "He wants to punish me, son. He's a faithless priest, who only knows violence."

Tom slapped Brodus. "Shut up, demon!"

"Whoa, Priest." Jericho grabbed Tom's shoulder. "Was that really necessary?"

Tom straightened and turned to Jericho. "Like I said, you need to leave."

Jericho looked over Tom's shoulder at Brodus, who smiled. "Ok. Ok. I'll step back. Get to work, Priest."

Jericho leaned back against the wall. *Dammit!*

Tom kneeled by the bed again. "All-powerful God, pardon all the sins of your unworthy servant. Give me constant faith and power so that, armed with the power of Your holy strength, I can attack this cruel, evil spirit in confidence and security."

"You're faithless, Padilla, faithless," Brodus said. "Take that trinket from under me, and I'll give you the fight you want."

Tom sprinkled holy water on Brodus' forehead. "The power of Christ compels you, you unclean spirit. Leave Wilma's body and return to the underworld where you belong."

"I belong here." Brodus squirmed as the holy water burned, and steam rose from his forehead. "I belong in here with Wilma. Just like your mother joined Desoto. Just like your grandmother joined my master. They liked it. They were whores for the underworld."

Tom flicked more holy water on Brodus, who sat up and screamed. He turned and backhanded Tom, who fell backward. Jericho pushed himself from up against the wall. He reached down and help Tom back to his knees.

Brodus spoke in Wilma's voice again. "He's killing me, Jericho. He's killing me. *You're* killing me."

"Dammit, continue, Tom," Jericho said.

Tom reached in his front pants pocket and pulled out a small gold crucifix. He put it in the palm of his hand and slapped it down on Brodus' forehead.

"You have no power here, demon." Tom pressed his hand harder. "In the name of the Lord, flee this realm. Flee this innocent woman. You and your kind were imprisoned in the underworld. Return there. Now!"

Brodus began to shake. His eyes glowed red. He coughed and opened his mouth as if he were about to leave Wilma's body. However, a burning sensation ran through Tom's hand. The crucifix began to glow, and it burned Tom and Brodus. They yelled out in pain.

Brodus kicked his legs, and the rope snapped that bound his waist. He turned to the side and chopped Tom in the neck, who jumped to his feet and grabbed his throat. Jericho put his hands on the back of Tom's shoulders to steady his friend. However, Brodus was free. The demon jumped in the air and kicked Tom in the head; he fell to the floor and crashed into Jericho, who was pushed against the wall. Tom stayed on the floor and struggled to get back up.

"It's just you and me again, Slayer." Brodus retreated into the dark corner. "You will pay for your stupidity."

Jericho reached back and pulled out his sword. "Don't make me do this, mother. Fight him. You're a Trident. I know you're in there."

"K-kill m-me s-s-son." Wilma's voice struggled to speak.

"Shut up, bitch." Brodus punched his head. "You and your son are mine now."

Brodus raised his arms. The wind inside the room picked up and small items drifted throughout. Jericho covered his face as a wooden chair smashed into the back of his head. Brodus pointed at the desk next to Jericho, and the top drawer opened. Five short and sharpened knives floated out. Brodus flicked his wrist, and one knife plunged into Jericho's right shoulder, causing him to drop the Sword of Caine. Brodus flicked his wrist again, and another knife shot into Jericho's other shoulder. The blade pinned Jericho to the wall.

Jericho's eyes glowed white. His sword shook and began to float into the air.

"Not so fast, Slayer," Brodus said, as he directed another

knife to stab Jericho in the stomach. "You will die here today."

Jericho broke away from the wall to bend over and put his hands over his stomach. When he looked up again, Brodus had maneuvered another knife right in front of Jericho's head. But Brodus quickly turned to the side to look at the cot. The crucifix began to float, and Tom grabbed it out of the windy air. Before Brodus could direct his power at the priest, Tom rose to his feet. He let the crucifix hanging from the beads, and it became a whip. Tom swung the whip with the crucifix at Brodus. The edge of the crucifix struck Brodus in the face, leaving a welt. Tom swung again. The crucifix left another welt on the other side of Brodus' face.

"Those match your other scars." Tom twirled the whip to swing again. "It's not like you were ever going to win a beauty contest anyway."

Brodus grunted. "Damn you, Priest!"

The wind stopped as Brodus dropped to his knees. Jericho also fell to all four and then pulled the knives out of his body. He sat back against the wall. *My slayer healing abilities won't heal me in time to help Tom. He's is on his own.*

Tom took a step toward Brodus, who jumped up with back stuck to the wall. He climbed backward until the top of his head hit the ceiling.

"Stay away from me, Padilla," Brodus said as his eyes glowed red.

A knife that Jericho pulled from his shoulder floated up and shot toward the back of Tom's head. However, Tom's eyes glowed white, and the blade stopped right as it reached Tom's head.

"Your powers are now my powers too, demon." Tom stepped to the side and brushed the knife out of the way. He reached down with both hands in his jacket pockets. When he pulled them out again, his brass knuckles were on his hands. "My turn."

Tom ran over and dove toward Brodus. He grabbed Brodus' legs and pulled the demon back down to the floor. He began to punch Brodus in the face. With each punch, a crucifix symbol, embedded in the brass knuckles, was left on Brodus' face. The demon screamed out, and Wilma's voice returned.

"K-kill me p-priest." Wilma managed to say. "H-He's w-weak now, but not g-gone."

"No!" Jericho held out his hand toward Tom but could barely move as held the wound in his stomach. "Don't do it, Thomas."

"H-He won't s-stop t-t-till you're de – "

"She's right," Brodus returned and grabbed Tom's throat with both hands. "Now, die."

Tom fell backward to the floor as Brodus got on top and mounted the priest. Brodus' eyes glowed red as he applied more pressure on Tom's neck. Jericho slowly crawled over, but Brodus took one hand off of Tom's throat and used his power to freeze the slayer. Tom's eyes rolled back and he stopped struggling.

"Stop this, mother," Jericho pleaded. "I know you're in there. Fight!"

Brodus turned to Jericho and smiled. "No, she's not. She's

dead."

Jericho stopped struggling to move as well. He believed the demon, which meant that he'd failed. Saving Tom or himself exited his mind as tears welled up in his eyes. Jericho allowed Brodus' power to push him back against the wall.

Suddenly, Tom's eyes popped back open. He shoved a vial of the yellow liquid, known as Detox, into Brodus' mouth. He then punched Brodus in the jaw, breaking the glass vial and releasing the fluid. Brodus tried spitting out the liquid but couldn't as the broken glass had prevented him from doing so. The demon fell to the side, grabbing his throat. He coughed as blood, and Detox traveled down his throat. Finally, Brodus rolled over on his back. The red glow in his eyes disappeared. He opened his mouth. Yellow smoke floated into the air and evaporated. He was gone.

Part IX

Brother VS Brother

Saint John's Catholic Church

Jericho crawled over, kneeled next Wilma, and took her hand. His slayer healing abilities had finally healed his wounds. A tear rolled down his face and mixed with the blood from the cut under his eye. A bloody tear fell to the floor. He kissed the back of Wilma's hand and then placed it against his forehead. Finally, a stream of tears ran down his face. *I'm so sorry, mom. None of this would have happened if you hadn't tried to find me. I've lost you twice now.*

Tom had recovered, walked over, and put his hand on Jericho's shoulder. Jericho snatched his shoulder away. Tom placed his hand on Jericho's shoulder again. This time, Jericho grabbed Tom's hand and tossed it to the side.

"This is your fault." Jericho stood. "You had to be the world-famous demon hunter, didn't you?"

"He was going to kill you *and me!*"

"I would have made that sacrifice."

"Well, I wouldn't have. And I didn't."

Jericho placed his hands on his hips. "You don't get it, do you, Priest? That was my mother."

"But that thing inside her wasn't."

"And so, you did what you do best." Jericho stood face-to-face with Tom. "They should call you the demon killer instead of the hunter."

"This is what we do, big guy. You knew this was a possibility."

"Not for my mother." Jericho pushed Tom's shoulder. "Or did she have to be Asian for you to give a crap whether she lived or died?"

Tom sighed and looked down at his shoulder. Jericho shoved. "Please, don't do that again."

"What…this? Jericho shoved Tom again.

Tom punched Jericho in the nose. Jericho staggered backward and smiled at the half-hearted punch. Jericho charged Tom, and they crashed through the wall and into the office next door. Jericho got up first as he landed on top of Tom. He reached down and grabbed Tom by his shirt collar and pulled him up. Jericho turned Tom around and grabbed him by the back of his shirt and his pants. He tossed Tom through the office door and into the hallway.

When Jericho stepped through the splintered door, he looked down, but Tom was gone. Jericho looked around and began to walk down the hall back into the main church.

"Come on, Priest," Jericho yelled as he looked around the church. "You've had this coming for years, my friend. Now, come and take it like a man."

Jericho walked past the first pew, where Tom was hiding. Tom popped up and punched Jericho in the back of the head. Jericho fell forward to the floor. He pushed himself back to his feet and turned around. Tom was gone again.

"Is that how you're gonna play this, Thomas?" Jericho slowly walked down the center aisle. "You're gonna hit and run like some chicken-shit?"

"Heads up!" Tom yelled out as he speared Jericho form behind. "I told you to watch your mouth in here."

They crashed into a pew and flipped it over. Jericho got to his feet, and Tom was gone again. Jericho picked up the long pew and tossed it across the church. The pew crashed into the upper pane-glass window and shattered it.

"We've gotta get out of here, Caine," Tom said as he looked down from the second floor. "You can't destroy this church."

"Why?" Jericho asked as he looked up and located Tom. "Because it was renamed for your daddy? Come down and fight me."

"I'll meet you outside."

Jericho walked faster as he headed for the front door. He walked out, and the police had set up a barricade around the church. Jericho walked down the steps to the sidewalk and turned around to face the entrance. He waited for Tom to come out, but the exorcist didn't follow.

"Fine." Jericho took a step back up the stairs. "We'll just have to finish this inside."

Tom appeared at the entrance of the church. He had on brass knuckles, and he pounded his fist into his other hand.

"I don't want to fight you, big guy," Tom said. "But if this is what you want, then so be it."

"I do, you self-righteous jackass." Jericho walked back up the steps. "And now, there's an audience."

Tom glanced around at the crowd that had gathered, who looked on from behind the police barricade. He ran down the stairs and threw a punch at Jericho, who ducked. Jericho then grabbed Tom by the hips and flipped the demon hunter in the air. Tom landed on his back on the concrete steps. Jericho turned and stomped on Tom's stomach. The air left Tom's body as he clutched his gut and breathed heavy. Jericho reached down, picked Tom up, and pressed Tom over his head. He tossed Tom down to the sidewalk, who cracked the side of his head on the ground. Blood drizzled from a gash on his head, down the side of his face.

Tom got up and wobbled to the side. He saw Jericho charging, but his eyesight was blurred. Tom threw a wild uppercut that connected to Jericho's chin. Jericho fell backward to the ground, and blood spewed from his mouth. Jericho looked up and swept Tom's legs, who fell to the floor next to Jericho. Jericho turned to the side and grabbed Tom's throat with both hands. Jericho began to squeeze as Tom's eyes bulged.

Downtown New York

Mobus stepped out of the elevator. He wiped the drool from his mouth and looked in all directions. The lights were dimmed except for the light emanating from the center of the room. He dragged in his injured foot across the hardwood floor and into the dining area. He stopped and looked around again. He grunted. Nothing. He grunted louder. Still nothing. He waved his hand and turned back toward the elevator.

"You give up too quickly, my friend." A voice echoed throughout the loft.

"Show self," Mobus said. "Not mood for games."

The ceiling lights popped on and exposed Thaden sitting in a corner chair. He sipped blood out of a wine glass.

Thaden held up his glass. "Drink?"

"Only brains."

"When my plans are complete." Thaden stood. "You and your guys can have all the brains you can eat. But *only* when the plan is complete."

Mobus cocked his head to the side. "What mean?"

"Some of your boys ate and killed one of my vampires." Thaden nodded toward the swinging kitchen door. "We're all on the same side, my friend."

Olaf walked into the room. He took out his guns, placed them on the dining table, and then sat. He didn't relinquish his gaze of Mobus.

Mobus grunted. "What is problem? Vamps dead brain is good as alive one."

Thaden grinned. "I understand that you think it's ok. But the more vampires you kill, the less I'll have to achieve my ultimate goal."

"Need tougher vamps then." Mobus' eyes moved back and forth from Thaden to Olaf. "Vamps weak."

Thaden sighed. "I keep you around because you control the rest of those deadheads. Don't make me regret that decision."

"Threat?" Mobus asked.

Thaden dropped his wine glass on the floor. "Let me put it another way."

Thaden ran toward Mobus and tackled him. They crashed through the dining room window and fell down several flights before crashing onto the patio on the sixtieth floor. The two began to move. Thaden looked up and saw Olaf peering down from the broken window. *Go do your job assassin.*

Thaden then looked over at Mobus, who had spewing from his mouth. He licked it, and turned to find Thaden already standing.

"You want fight?" Mobus asked as he balled his fist.

"Is that a serious question?" Thaden asked. "Bring it on!"

Mobus charged Thaden. They rolled over the patio furniture and into the swimming pool. Thaden's werewolf fur appeared on his arm, as he grabbed Mobus by the throat and tossed him out of the pool and over the bar on the patio. Thaden pulled himself out of the pool and ran toward Mobus, who picked up a bar stool by the legs and swung it. He cracked Thaden in the face, sending the half-breed creature flying across the deck and through a glass door. Thaden shook off the broken glass. Before he could locate Mobus, the zombie's fist struck Thaden in the jaw. Thaden crashed into the wall-mounted television and slid to the floor. The television, a fifty-five-inch flat screen, fell and smashed on top of Thaden's head. The man and the woman who lived in the loft ran inside their bedroom and locked the door.

Mobus walked to the front door of the loft. He opened it, and two zombies, both the same in height and weight, entered. One was Latino, and the other was white. They walked over and picked up Thaden by the arms. They slammed him into the wall and waited for Mobus to make his way over.

Thaden was groggy as his head drooped to the floor. A string of bloody saliva hung from his mouth. Mobus grabbed Thaden by the hair and lifted his head. Mobus cocked his head to the side so he could stare into Thaden's face.

"You not boss anymore," Mobus said. "Mobus run things now."

"Y-You will never be the leader." Thaden tried to snatch his head away from Mobus' grip. "Because you don't have this."

Thaden's fingernails grew longer on his werewolf hand. He ripped his arm away from the Latino zombie and jammed his fingers into the zombie's eyes. He reached behind his back and pulled out the Takara Dagger.

"No!" Mobus grabbed Thaden's arm. "Mobus boss now."

160

Thaden head-butted Mobus and knocked the zombie leader backward and off-balance. Thaden then jammed the dagger into the other zombie's throat that held his other arm. He twisted the blade and yanked it out, ripping off the zombie's head. The zombie fell and released Thaden, who then pointed the dagger at the blinded zombie. A golden beam of light shot out of the dagger and pounded the zombie in the chest, sending him spiraling into the far wall. The zombie stood and rubbed his smoking chest. Then, he looked up at Thaden and back to his chest. The zombie began to glow bright gold: his body began to dissolve into a puddle of black liquid.

Thaden looked down and enjoyed the carnage he'd caused. One zombie was headless on the floor. The other was liquidated. Thaden searched for Mobus, who had managed to sneak out during the ruckus. Thaden ran out of the front door, but he was tackled as soon as he entered the hall. The dagger fell out of his hand and slid down the hallway. Mobus got to his feet first and dove to the ground to retrieve the weapon.

Mobus stood and pointed the dagger at Thaden, who slowly got back to his feet. "I told you. Mobus run things now."

"You're as stupid as you are ambitious." Thaden's werewolf fur disappeared. "You don't have what it takes to wield the dagger."

Thaden's eyes glowed red and then bright gold. The Takara Dagger glowed as well. Mobus dropped the dagger as his hand began to smoke, and looked down at his bruised hand.

Thaden walked down the hall. "The dagger and I have

become one. And it will stay that way until I die. You're an idiot, zombie. It's a shame too, because I liked you, Mobus. But today, you have proven yourself to be my enemy."

Thaden held out his hand, and the dagger floated in the air. It sailed across the hall and into Thaden's grip. Mobus eyes widened as he turned to run toward the elevator. But with his limp, he couldn't run fast. Thaden pointed the dagger at Mobus and fired a golden beam of light. The beam struck Mobus in the back. He fell face-first to the floor. His body glowed gold for a few seconds, and then the glow subsided. He turned over and began to scoot backward on his butt toward the elevator.

"Hmm," Thaden said as he continued to walk toward Mobus. "I guess you really were special, after all. It took only one shot to dispatch the other zombie. Let's see if you'll survive another one."

Mobus held out his hands. "Noooo!"

Thaden shot another golden beam of light from the dagger. The blast hit Mobus in his outstretched hands first; then, the golden glow spread over his entire body. He began to hemorrhage. He fell on his back and kicked his legs in the air: he jerked one last time until his body began to dissolve into a black puddle.

Thaden stepped over the puddle and pushed the elevator button. "Now for the rest."

When the elevator reached the basement, Thaden gripped the dagger tightly and prepared to do battle with the remaining zombies. The doors opened. Olaf stood waiting with a double-barreled shotgun. He stepped to the side and motioned to the black-bloody mess he'd just created. Three bodies with missing heads, from shotgun blasts, lay on the floor.

"I figured this was your next stop, boss," Olaf said. "I knew if you killed Mobus, the rest had to go as well."

"I like the way you think, Mr. Sader." Thaden returned the dagger to the sheath in the small of his back. "Now, let's go finish planning the demise of the Death Brothers."

Saint John's Church

Tom's eyes rolled back, and his tongue hung out his mouth. Jericho loosened his grip and Tom's throat and prepared to punch Tom. Suddenly, the sky turned dark. Lightning filled the sky, and thunder sounded out. The passersby's stopped moving. Everyone in the vicinity was frozen. The streetlight blinked on and off before staying on permanently. Jericho stood and looked around the area. *What in the hell is going on here? Jesus! It's gotta be the Hangman. He waited till Tom, and I tried to kill each other, and now he's making his move.*

Tom held his throat as he got back to his feet. He looked around as well before glaring at Jericho. He pushed the slayer in the chest and got in his fight stance once again.

"Enough!" A booming voice echoed throughout. "This ends now!"

Jericho

A bright light flashed. When it disappeared, Jericho found himself in another dark space. He knew he wasn't outside anymore, or around anybody. *This is just like when Harold possessed my body. But that can't happen again. Can it?*

A white ball of light floated down from above Jericho's head. "It's not that, Caine."

"What is this, then?" Jericho asked.

"You two have made a mess of things." The light stopped right in front of Jericho's face. "We are here to remedy that."

"Who is *we?*"

The light expanded until it was Jericho's size, and it transformed into a man with short blonde hair, a chiseled jaw, and a grizzled look. He was as muscular as Jericho.

"I am Stephen Dupree, Slayer," he said. "And, I'll assume that you are supposed to be the new me."

"Holy crap!" Jericho took a step back. "How, and why, are *you* here?"

Tom

"My name is Patrick Dupree, Thomas. And I am here to help right the ship."

Tom studied the medium-sized brunette. "This can't be."

"Yes, it can."

"Who sent you, the angels?"

164

"Arellos sent us. He felt it was time for us to meet."

Tom laughed. "He doesn't like dealing with that meathead Jericho. I can see why now."

"Listen." Patrick stretched out his arms to the side. "I know Steph – I mean Jericho, can be tough to get along with. But Stephen was the same way. We fought all the time. But I knew, for us to continue for as long as we did, I'd have to learn to accept him and his many...*many* flaws."

Jericho

"Jericho, Tom was your first true friend," Stephen said. "Deep down, you know he did everything in his power to save your mother."

"I'm tired of his holier-than-thou attitude." Jericho folded his arms. "He can break the rules when it suits him, but let someone else try to do it, then he breaks out his priest's collar and lectures you to death."

"Ha. Ha. Ha. Patrick was a man of faith too. It was a perfect balance for my off-the-cuff shenanigans. The last incarnation of the Death Brothers failed because they had too much in common but didn't really care for each other. You love Thomas Padilla, though. And he loves you. Your mother's sacrifice wasn't to turn you two against each other. It was to show you that you can overcome anything."

Jericho inhaled deeply and exhaled even deeper. "He *is* the only person that can deal with my sense of humor."

"The angels hate it your sense of humor, by the way."

Jericho erupted in laughter. "I'm sure they do."

Tom

"You have found love with Ms. Taki, Thomas. You have found peace with your faith. And you have redeemed your family's name when you destroyed Desoto. Jericho is still searching for those things. So, you must try to understand how he feels about the death of his mother."

Tom dropped and shook his head. "I never looked at it that way, especially when that huge fist smashed into my face."

"Try to be a little more patient with him, Tom."

"I haven't been patient *enough*?"

Patrick laughed. "The angels think you have exhibited more patience than any human that's ever been created."

Tom smiled. "It's good to know that someone else has noticed."

"I've said it once, and I'll say it again." Patrick put his hand on Tom's shoulder. "You two have the potential to be the best iteration of the Death Brothers…even better than us."

Jericho

"Thank you, Stephen," Jericho said. "I will be sure to keep your legacy sacred."

"I know you will, Slayer. Now it's time for me to go."

Tom

"Thank you, Patrick," Tom said. "Your guidance and wisdom will not go to waste."

"It's why I love checking in on you, Thomas. Goodbye. And good luck."

Daylight appeared, and the sky returned to its calm, blue appearance. The people on the street began to move again as the police continued to hold them at bay. Tom and Jericho stared at each other. Tom put out his hand to shake Jericho's hand. Jericho took a step toward Tom and slapped Tom's hand out of the way.

Jericho wrapped his arms around Tom. "Brothers hug it out after a fight."

Tom hugged Jericho as well. "I'm sorry about your mother, big guy."

"Thanks, Thomas," Jericho said. "Now, to the problem at hand. We have a rogue angel out there pulling a bunch of strings to get rid of us."

"And the funny thing is," Tom began. "She's not even our biggest threat. Thaden has the Takara Dagger. He has an assassin, a vengeful mad scientist, and vampires at his side. *They* want us all dead."

"After the day I've had, I say, let's go give them what they want then."

"Agreed. But we must tread lightly, big guy. I'm getting the sense that something is still missing from this story. But right now, let's go to the hospital. Susie is awake."

"Wow!" Jericho slapped Tom on the back. "I'm glad to hear that, buddy. Let's go."

Part X

Together Again

Hospital

Tom rushed through the hospital, trying to avoid running into anyone. Jericho followed him but kept a certain distance. Tom opened the room door to see Alexander sitting in a chair next to Susie's bed. Susie was awake and smiling. When she recognized Tom, she began to cry. Tom walked over and hugged her. They kissed, and he stroked her long black hair.

"I've missed you so much, woman," Tom said.

Susie pressed her forehead against Tom's. "I don't remember much, but I knew I couldn't let her hurt you."

"You saved us, honey." Tom glanced the back of his hand across her cheek. "But don't ever do that again. I was so scared."

Susie smiled as more tears rolled down her face. "Deal."

"Jesus, Tom," Jericho said as he entered the room. "This is a hospital, not a hotel room."

Alexander walked over, shook Jericho's hand, and glared back at Tom and Susie. "This is why we do what we do, Caine."

Jericho smiled. "I don't know about you, wizard. But I do it to borrow pickup trucks."

"Since when do they call stealing, borrowing?" Alexander asked.

"I see you've been listening to the priest." Jericho patted Alexander on the back. "But borrowing, stealing, it's all the same when people owe you."

Alexander laughed. "I was told you'd say that too."

"Oh my God," Susie lifted her head. "Is that Jericho Caine over there?"

"In the flesh." Jericho walked over and hugged Susie. "They told me your long hair was a disguise to keep you safe."

"Ha. Ha. Ha." Susie slapped Jericho's arm. "Same ole' Caine."

The three heroes found chairs to sit down around Susie's bed. They updated each other on current events. Jericho and Tom didn't mention their fight. They also wanted to dismiss Alexander. He'd done more than they wanted him to do.

Jericho put two fingers to his temple and looked at Tom. *We have to let the wizard go. He's gotta get back to his new family.*

We'd be letting go of a huge asset, big guy.

This is our fight. Besides, we'll need him for when the Hangman shows up again.

Tom twisted his lips. *Sadly, I agree.*

"Jericho is right, Alexander," Tom began. "You should go and be with your family."

Susie's eyes opened wider. "Did you guys just do that telepathy thing you told me about? We were in the middle of a conversation. It's a cool trick, but kinda rude."

"I can stay to help," Alexander said. "This isn't a world-ending situation, but it can become perilous."

"We'll do our best without you, wizard." Jericho patted Alexander's leg. "We'll need you for when the Hangman returns."

"That's right, Alexander," Tom began. "You will definitely be needed down the line. This situation exists between Jericho and me. So, we'll handle it."

"Are you sure?" Alexander asked.

"Wait a minute." Jericho smacked the side of his head. "I forgot to tell you guys something. When Brodus had set off the supernatural alarms at the church, I was in a magic shop a few blocks away. It's how I got there so quickly."

Jericho's story

I'd just arrived from Rhode Island. I was confused about what was going on with a woman named Sarah that I'd been with. I thought she was part of a plot from the Hangman to throw me off. So, when I got back to New York, I knew if I wanted answers, I'd get them from Tony at Tony's Magic Shop. He and I have shared information about the supernatural with each other over the years.

I parked one of my borrowed trucks and went into the shop.

It was always empty at that time of day. As soon as Tony spotted me, he ran toward the back. I knew something was going on, so I chased him and, fortunately, I caught him trying to run out the back door, the one which leads to the alley.

I grabbed him by the shirt collars and pressed him up against the wall. "What's going on, Tony? Why are you running from me?"

"Your name is mud, Slayer," he said. "Anyone seen talking to you will be marked."

"Marked? Why? And by whom?"

"Supposedly, there's a female angel who has dealings with your old pal, the Hangman. Word is, they are also in league with some new guy named Thaden. And some guy from the Frankenstein linage."

"I know a little bit about that already." I pressed him against the wall harder. "Tell me something I don't know."

"The angel only wants the priest out of the way, but the Frankenstein guy and his monster want you all dead...including the angel and the Hangman."

"Who told you this?"

Tony looked around. "Let's go inside first. We're exposed out here."

"We're not going anywhere." I slapped him. "Now tell me what you know, Tony. You know me. And that means you know what I'll do to you if you don't spill guts."

"I'm not a vampire. You can't hurt me."

"Wrong. I won't kill you. But I will hurt you. Then I'll burn

down your shop."

Tony stared into my eyes. I was serious, and I believe he knew it. I lowered him back to the ground, and I followed him back inside the shop.

"Ok. We're off the streets," I began. "Now, who is your source? And what does the Hangman have to do with this?"

"His name is Dr. Grundy, a brilliant guy. He was the other doctor's assistant. He has disappeared, though. And from what he told me, the Hangman has his own agenda. The angel just needed him to conjure some type of spell."

"Hmm. That explains a few things. But I need to reach out to the Hangman. And I'm gonna need your help."

Tony and I searched the magic shop for the ingredients to cast a spell. I needed to talk to the Hangman. I decided that I was going to confront him alone to find out what spell he'd cast for the angel. I also wanted to know what his plans were now that he had the Power Ring. I knew he wouldn't talk to anyone else but me. Also, I wanted to know why he killed BA.

We found what we needed to send him a message. I could only use the spell to write a message on something in his vicinity. If he read it or not, I wouldn't know unless he showed up. However, it was a chance I was willing to take.

"What was your message?" Tom asked.

"It simply said, *tomorrow at noon, where we first met,*" Jericho replied.

"You think he got it?" Alexander's eyes widened. "And more

importantly, do you think he'll show?"

"Well, we only have a few hours," Jericho said. "Because tomorrow is today. And we need to get to Tanner, Illinois, in a hurry. That is where I first encountered the Hangman."

"It's settled then." Alexander stood. "You need me, not only to get you there in time, but to help deal with the Hangman as well."

"Count me in too." Susie sat up in the bed and pulled out her Ivee. "Physically, there's nothing wrong with me, except for a little atrophy. And I'm not worried about that too much."

"Are you sure, baby?" Tom stood and leaned in closer to Susie. "I know you're tough, but I just got you back."

"Tom," Susie said. "I've known how to kick ass long before I met you. I'll be alright. Besides, Caine isn't the only one who knows how to heal himself."

They all looked at each other and nodded. They didn't expect to face the Hangman so soon, but they knew they had to see where things stood with the half-demon. They already had to deal with Sariel and Thaden. However, the Hangman was a problem they wanted to address separately.

Tanner, Illinois

Around noon, a portal opened inside the old barn. The heroes stepped out and surveyed the scene. Jericho walked over to the entrance and opened the barn door, which fell off the hinges. They laughed as Jericho leaned the door up against the wall. They all turned around and looked for something to sit on.

Tom threw bales of hay from the top level of the barn, and they all sat. Jericho didn't know what to expect, so he sat to relax, but stayed focused on the entrance. *Doesn't look as if anyone has lived here for years. The wheat and corn fields outside are all dead.* The red paint on the barn had peeled, and rusted tools that remained hung throughout the barn were rusted.

"So, wait." Susie broke the silence. "Are you saying that his spell is the reason I'm awake?"

"I'm not sure," Tom said. "But if I had to guess, it's definitely appears that way. Those pink clouds had to have come from somewhere."

"Tom's right," Alexander cut in. "Speaking as wizard, what you all have described, is the work of very powerful spell."

Susie fiddled with her fingers. "I'll be that sucka, thinks he gets a free pass now?"

"Well, if he shows up alone," Jericho began. "We can assume he's *not* our enemy."

"Jesus!" Tom stomped his foot. "It doesn't matter if he's come to fight us or not, Caine. He killed BA. Period."

"I can't believe we're still debating this subject." Alexander cut in. "There are only two options. We either fight *just* him. Or he shows up with the angel and Thaden, which makes our job even more difficult."

"I'm not even going to argue anymore." Tom stood and folded his arms. "Caine, you're either with us or go the hell home."

"Of course, I'm with you guys," Jericho said. "I'm just saying that this is a delicate situation."

"I'm sorry, big guy." Susie stood as well. "But these guys are right."

Jericho twisted his lips. "Oh, there's a shocker, Ms. Taki. I didn't expect you *not* to disagree with your boyfriend."

"You know that's not true, you big dumb bastard." She frowned. "I think for myself. And defeating the Hangman has got to be just as important as defeating the others."

"But why?" Jericho pleaded. "He was murdered as a human. And then, as if that weren't enough, his wife and son were murdered. He is just as much of a victim in this as anybody."

"He's killed tons of people, Caine." Susie walked over and stared up into Jericho's face. "But most importantly, he killed BA, our ally and our friend."

"Let's get one thing straight." Jericho folded his arms. "BA was not *my* friend. And I'm not so sure angels are as good and pure as you all make them out to be."

Alexander stood. "I can't listen to this anymore." He turned and walked toward the barn entrance. "Wait a minute. You guys smell that?"

They all rushed over to the opening. They looked over to the house and saw white smoke rising into the air from the other side. They began to walk toward the house. Suddenly, a bolt of light struck the ground in front of them, causing dirt and smoke to rise. Jericho unsheathed his sword, Tom pulled out his pole, Alexander's staff appeared in his hand, and Susie reached in the small of her back for her nunchucks.

The smoke cleared, and the Hangman, almost seven feet tall, and wearing a black robe, appeared. He had his hooked staff in one hand, and the Power Ring glowed bright pink in the other.

"Sorry," the Hangman began. "But I can't let you guys pass."

"Whoa, Hangy." Jericho stepped forward. "I asked you here to talk, not fight."

"You have a good memory, Caine." The Hangman scanned the area. "I almost forgot about this place."

"I was hoping to remind you of a more peaceful time between us," Jericho said.

The Hangman nodded toward the others. "And do they feel as you do?"

Jericho glared slightly to the side at the others. He knew he had to choose his words carefully, so he motioned for the others to lower their weapons. However, he also noticed that the Power Ring on the Hangman's hand began to blink. *He's stalling us. I'd better push the issue and see where we stand.*

"Ok," Jericho began. "They've lowered their weapons. But we need some answers from you, my friend."

"Answers?" The Hangman asked. "From me?"

"Yes," Jericho responded. "Why did you kill BA? There's gotta be a logical reason, Hangy."

The Hangman's eyes rotated from the anxious and curious faces that stared back at him. "Well, I killed BA...because I could."

Jericho's mouth fell open. "No. That can't be right. That can't

177

be the real reason."

"Enough of this." Alexander raised his staff again. "There's no reasoning with this monster."

Alexander swung his staff, but the Hangman blocked it with his hooked staff and backhanded Alexander, who sailed across the lawn and into the withered wheat field. Susie swung her nunchucks and smacked the Hangman in the face. A blue electric pulse erupted from the contact. However, the Hangman barely flinched and kicked Susie in the stomach. She bent over, and then he brought his knee her in the forehead. She was knocked back a few feet and landed on to the ground. Tom then sprang into action with his pole. He jabbed the sharpened edge at the Hangman several times, but the Hangman either ducked or stepped to the side. Finally, the Hangman grabbed Tom's pole and tossed Tom through the air. He crashed through the sidewall of the house.

Jericho looked down at the Hangman's ring again. It stopped flashing and glowed a continuous bright pink.

"What's wrong, Caine?" The Hangman asked as he noticed the disappointment in Jericho's face. "Didn't like my answer?"

Jericho looked over at the house and then back at the Hangman. "What are you doing out here, Hangy? You're up to something, and it wasn't just to meet with me."

"And they said you were the dumb one." The Hangman grunted. "In return for helping to bring a monster to life, I get to free my wife and son. As a bonus, I'll lay waste to Purgatory while I'm at it."

"Free?" Jericho cocked his head to the side. "Aren't they in Heaven right now?"

The Hangman glanced over at the house then back to Jericho. "I have assurances that they are in Purgatory as we speak. Waiting for me to reunite with them."

"That doesn't sound like it's on the up-and-up, Hangy." Jericho shook his head. "How are you even able to do this?"

The Hangman smiled. "It's my payment from your little angel girlfriend. And like I said, destroying Purgatory for the all the time I spent in that dump, will be a bonus."

"Destroy?" Jericho's eyes tightened. "Is that really necessary?"

The Hangman planted his staff into the ground. "Yes. I'm going to destroy any-and-everything in that place, including the angel that guards it."

"He's telling the truth." Alexander emerged from the wheat field. "The smoke is from a spell that opened a portal on the other side of the house. I can see it from here."

Alexander ran toward the portal. The Hangman pointed his ring and fired. The pink beam of light crashed to the ground in front of Alexander. The explosion sent the wizard flying back into the wheat field.

Jericho took off, running toward the fallen wizard. "Alexander!"

Tom recovered with one of his brass knuckles on his fists. He ran out of the front door of the house and punched the Hangman in the jaw. Thunder sounded out with the contact, and the half-demon was sent crashing to the ground. The Hangman pushed himself up to one knee and held his jaw. He looked over at Tom's fist and saw the crucifixes that were engraved on the brass knuckles still glowing.

"You're really starting to bug me, Priest," the Hangman said as he got back to his feet. "I can zap you out of existence in the blink of an eye."

Tom nodded. "There's the demon that I know. You may have Caine fooled, but I know that this is the real Hangman."

Susie recovered and stood beside Tom. "And me."

New York

The elevator opened. Olaf took a deep breath and stepped out. When he entered the living room, he sat on the white leather couch and put up his feet on the glass coffee table.

Dr. Ranken entered the room from the kitchen. "I see that you like to make yourself comfortable in other people's homes, Mr. Sader."

Olaf leaned further back and clasped his hands behind his head. "Is there a problem, Doc?"

"It's rude," Dr. Ranken said.

"Come now, doctor," Thaden said as he entered the room from behind Dr. Ranken. "Be nice to our guest, especially one, who is loyal as Mr. Sader."

The wind blew open the double glass patio doors. Dr. Ranken

and Olaf covered their faces until the breeze was done. When they looked up again, Sariel stood outside on the patio. She entered the living room and glared at everyone.

"Gear up," she said. "We've got a date in Illinois."

"Says who?" Thaden stood and placed his hands behind his back. "There's nothing in Illinois that concerns us."

"*They* are there." Sariel frowned. "We could wipe them out all at once, including the Hangman."

"And why should we?" Thaden paced. "The Hangman will deal with the Death Brothers, the wizard, and the Taki woman. We have no quarrels with him…just yet."

"You still don't get it, do you?" Sariel folded her arms. "We have to make sure that the demon enters the portal to Purgatory. I need him to go through it to get rid of him. A battalion of angels awaits him on the other side, including the archangel Gabriel. He wants revenge on the demon for killing his *protégé*. Even with the Power Ring, the Hangman can't handle that many angels."

Dr. Ranken held up his finger. "And what makes you think they can stop him from entering."

"He has a soft spot for Caine," Sariel said. "They will use that to their advantage. We must go there and make sure he won't be hindered from entering."

"You set him up," Thaden said. "So, what's going to stop you from setting us up as well?"

Sariel smiled. "I see you're feeling bold while you have the dagger. You think you're going to pick up the pieces after they fight it out? And what if they win? You'll still have to deal with the Sword of Cain and a powerful wizard. But, if we showed up and helped the Hangman go through the portal, we get rid of him, and hopefully, take out the others all at once."

Thaden sat next to Olaf. "You want us to put our plans in danger and risk pissing off the demon? I see no scenario where we come out of this unscathed if we go."

"What if I can guarantee you the Power Ring after Cromwell is defeated?" She asked.

"You can do that?" Thaden asked.

"How do you think all of this has come about in the first place, Thaden?" She smiled and put a foot up the table. "I am the reason the Death Brothers exist, the reason you are even alive, and the reason you enjoy the company of Mr. Sader. I kept my word and delivered an undead army to you. Sadly, you've either killed them or gotten them killed."

"What about me?" Dr. Ranken asked.

Sariel turned to Dr. Ranken. "I haven't forgotten about you, doctor. I promised you vengeance on Death Brothers. But now, I'm willing to let you put an end to both of their lives."

Thaden tapped his lip with his finger. "I still don't know what your end-game is. But you *have* delivered on all your promises so far."

She pointed to Thaden. "And now I will deliver anther promise. I will get you the most powerful weapon in existence. But I'll need your help to do it."

Thaden glared at Dr. Ranken and Olaf, and then back at Sariel. "You've got a deal."

"Great!" Sariel walked back out to the balcony and sprouted her wings. "Follow me."

Sariel launched herself into the air and flew away. Thaden stood and reached behind his back. He pulled out the Takara Dagger and stared at his reflection in the golden blade.

"The thing is," Thaden began. "She actually thinks she's gonna live through this."

Olaf laughed. "I was hoping you'd gut her while she was talking."

"Don't worry, my friend," Thaden said. "She'll get hers. And once we make sure the Hangman goes through the portal, we won't need the Power Ring. We'll let the angels keep it. All we'll need to do is kill the others and let the angels deal with the demon. Then we'll still have the most powerful weapon on earth, the Takara Dagger, *and* the Sword of Caine."

Tanner, Illinois

"Enough of this." The Hangman held his fist in the air, and the Power Ring began to glow bright pink. "You pesky humans are like a pebble in my shoe."

The sky darkened as more clouds moved in. Lightning flashed inside the newer clouds. Suddenly, bolts of lightning rained down and landed a few feet in front of the heroes. They dove and leaped to safety in each direction to avoid being hit.

"Back to the barn." Tom grabbed Susie's arm as they ran toward the barn. "We'll be safe there."

A bolt of light crashed down in front of the couple, separating and catapulting them in different directions. Susie landed closer to the barn, and she continued to crawl inside. Tom landed on his back near the house. He got back to his feet and entered from the hole that he'd blown through earlier.

"I need to go find Tom." Jericho patted Alexander on the back. "Are you good here?"

"Give me a second," Alexander said as he held up his staff. "Vis ager (force field). I think I can hold out until you guys come up with a plan."

A light blue bubble surrounded Alexander's body. Jericho nodded at the wizard and took off running. He glanced at the Hangman as he ran by. A bolt of light pounded the ground at Jericho's heels. The force of the lightning blast and his momentum caused him to leap through the front door of the house. He rolled on the floor until out of the Hangman's sight.

Tom crawled through the rubble on the floor. He ducked and made sure he couldn't be seen by the Hangman as he made his way over to Jericho. Jericho was out of breath, and Tom's forehead was cut.

"How long are we going to hide in here?" Tom asked. "It's time to end this, big guy. That's not the guy you used to know. You're not giving it your all."

"What in the hell are you talking about, Tom?" Jericho wiped blood from underneath his nose. "If you haven't noticed, I'm bleeding too."

"Please." Tom's forehead crumpled. "I've seen you endure more than this and get back up. Why are you still giving this guy a pass?"

"I'm not." Jericho shoved Tom's shoulder. "He's tough!"

"So what? You're Jericho Caine, the vampire slayer. You have the Sword of Caine. I've never seen you this hesitant before to get into a fight."

"He could wipe us off the map with that ring."

"Then why hasn't he then?"

"Because he doesn't want to kill us like I've been trying to tell you. He's pulling his punches too."

"Ok. I agree. Are you happy now? But Caine, we have to use that to our advantage. We just can't leave Alexander out there to do battle with a demon wielding the Power Ring."

"I know." Jericho sighed. "I know. Is your telepathy still working, or is your brain too scrambled?"

Tom stared into Jericho's face and put his finger to his temple. *I think so. Why?*

Jericho's eyes squinted as he concentrated. *Just hang with me for a little while longer.*

They had to jump back to their feet and dove out of the way, as a rusted green tractor crashed through the side of the house. Jericho walked out and saw the Hangman standing over Alexander, whose force field was gone. The Hangman was preparing to ram the sword of the hooked staff into the wizard's chest. Jericho launched his sword toward the Hangman, and it stuck in the ground next to the demon.

The Hangman looked at the sword and turned back toward the house. "Caine. Why are you doing this? Why are you and the rest of these humans trying to stop me from being with my family?"

Jericho walked down the porch steps with his arms out. "You just can't pull your family out of Heaven just because you miss them. It's not right, or everyone would be able to do it."

"I'm not everybody, in case you haven't noticed, Slayer," the Hangman said.

Jericho looked at Alexander and motioned both his head and his eyes to the side. He then called back the Sword of Caine to his hand. Surprisingly, he sheathed the sword and put up his hands as he continued to walk toward the Hangman.

"I get it, big man," Jericho began. "You're pissed. You think you didn't deserve this. But there a lot of people, who didn't deserve their fate. Pain is a part of life."

The Hangman dropped his head, and the hooked staff fell to his feet. He didn't notice that Alexander had gotten up and wandered away. Tom walked down the porch steps and stood a few feet behind Jericho. Susie joined Tom as they looked on.

The sound of thunder snapped the Hangman out of his trance. He looked over at the house, and he frowned as thunder rattled again. He opened his fist, and the hooked staff floated off the ground and back to his hand.

"Where's the wizard?" The Hangman demanded. "He doesn't know what he's about to do."

The Hangman waved his hand across the air. A powerful wind blew Jericho, Tom, and Susie off their feet to the ground. The Hangman walked quickly to the side of the house.

"No!" The Hangman held up his hand. "That portal can only be used once. If you destroy it, I'll never see my family again."

Alexander looked back at a large glowing white doorway. He'd stuck his staff halfway inside of it. The other heroes had made their way to the side of the house and surrounded the Hangman. Alexander surveyed their faces. Tom and Susie nodded their heads in agreement.

Only Jericho's facial expression seemed neutral. *We shouldn't let Hangy interfere with the natural order of life and death by allowing him to take back his family. At the same time, we're gonna have a pissed-off demon to deal with, armed with the Power Ring, if we stop him.*

"Wait!" Jericho finally broke the silence. "There's gotta be another way."

"There is no other way, Caine," the Hangman said. "The best thing for you to do is step aside and allow me to enter that portal...or else."

Sweat poured down Jericho's face. His eyes swayed from everyone in the field, who seemed to be frozen. No one wanted to make a hasty move.

Jericho's nose began to bleed again as he strained and looked at Tom. *I will distract him while you get the wizard to open another portal to someplace else. As far away from here as possible.*

Tom fought the headache that was quickly forming because the fight had taken a toll on his use of telepathy. *If you do this, there is no coming back. He will know you helped.*

I know. But it's time I put all doubts aside and end this.

Jericho dropped his sword and spread out his arms. He walked slowly over to the Hangman, who didn't take his eyes off Alexander.

"Listen, Hangy." Jericho slowly approached and got the Hangman's attention. "You know I feel your pain, and I know how much you want to be with your family again. But if we allow you to do this, will you leave the ring and Earth forever?"

"You know I can't do that, Caine," the Hangman said. "I have enemies that will never let me and my family live in peace."

"Well, you have to give us something." Jericho nodded. "We can't just give you everything you want."

The Hangman dropped his head. "The debate over. I can and will have it all."

The Hangman lifted his hooked staff and prepared to swing. The Sword of Caine quickly levitated back into Jericho's hand. Susie began whipping around her nunchucks, and Tom's grip around his pole tightened.

Susie leaped into the air and came down, swinging her nunchucks. The Hangman blocked them with his staff and kicked Susie in the chest, causing her to sail back to the dirt. The action allowed Tom to stab the knife of his pole into the Hangman's shoulder. The Hangman snatched out the poll and backhanded Tom. Tom was knocked backward and crashed landed on his back. Jericho looked over at Tom, who was drowsy and had dropped his weapon. Jericho then launched toward the Hangman with the Sword of Caine. Their weapons clashed off each other, and sparks flew.

They swung their weapons again, and they met face to face with their weapons, stuck together between them.

"I never wanted to fight you, Caine." The Hangman exposed his sharpened yellow teeth. "But you leave me no choice."

"I didn't want to fight you ei – "

The Hangman spat a yellow venom in Jericho's eyes, and he pushed Jericho to the ground. The venom stung. Jericho tried wiping his eyes, but his vision was blurred, and he could only hear Alexander yelling his name. He cleared one eye as the other eye was sealed. He held up his hand to stop Alexander, but it was too late. The wizard pulled his staff out of the portal and pointed it at the Hangman.

"Pulsus (pulse)." Alexander shot a barely visible ball of energy at the Hangman. "Take that, you bastard."

The Hangman's eyes glowed red as he waved his hand and knocked the pulse to the ground. "Ha. Ha. Ha. Stupid wizard. You'll never learn."

The Hangman pointed his ring at Alexander and prepared to fire. However, Susie jumped on his back and cuffed her hand around the Hangman's forehead. The blue energy she used to absorb supernatural abilities flowed from her hands to the Hangman's head. He fell to one knee with her still on his back. The Power Ring began to glow dark pink, and the glow covered his body. The energy catapulted Susie several feet across the field. She hit hard on the ground, leaving her unconscious.

The Hangman peered at Tom. "I can see why you like her, Priest. She's tough. But enough of this."

The Power Ring continued to glow, and the dark pink energy remained surrounding the Hangman. He walked toward the bright white tunnel, which was slowly shrank.

"It's closing." The Hangman picked up the pace. "You people are wasting my time."

The Hangman began to run toward the portal, and Alexander shot continuous pulses. They bounced off the dark pink force field. Tom launched his pole at the Hangman, which banked off the force field and stuck into the ground. Jericho recovered. He knew he was their last best hope. He dove in the air with his sword out in front and struck the Hangman in the back of the head. The force of the collision knocked Jericho and the Hangman to the ground. The sword of Caine was dislodged from Jericho's hand and landed a few feet away.

The Hangman, down on all four, shook his head rapidly and looked up at the portal. It continued to close. He got to his feet and began to sprint toward it.

"Nooo!" A voice yelled from above.

Part X: Together Again

The Hangman dove toward the portal. He looked up and saw Sariel descend from the sky just as his head entered the glowing white light. However, it was too late as the Hangman's entire body disappeared inside the portal. The portal then shrank to the size of a coin and vanished.

The Final Chapter

"**S**ariel." Jericho stood and called his sword back to his hand as Sariel hovered. "I should have known you'd try to stop this. But you're too late."

Alexander walked over and stood to the right of Jericho with his staff at his side.

"You know, Caine." Sariel landed and interlocked her fingers behind her back. "It has only dawned on me now that selecting you as a would-be suitor was a huge mistake. You're only in love with being the slayer. And you will ever let anyone get as close to you as the demon hunter."

"You're wrong about one thing," Jericho said. "I'm not *in love* with anything or anyone. But one thing's for sure, it would have never been *you*."

"You weren't saying that the other night." She countered.

Jericho grinned "That was until I found out you were a low down, stinky, filthy, double-crossing angel."

Alexander's eyes widened. "Whoa, Caine. That's a little harsh."

"Trust me," Jericho said. "I was thinking of something way worse to say."

Jericho looked around to find the rest of the team. Tom had run over to check on Susie, who was still unconscious. *Come on, Priest. Time to get back on the clock.*

"Where'd you send the demon?" Sariel asked. "I knew if you all were still alive, that couldn't have been the correct portal."

"To another dimension," Alexander said. "It'll be a while before we see him again."

"So, this is the way its gonna end, huh?" Sariel's eyes moved back and forth from Jericho to Alexander. "And all I ever wanted to do was kill the priest. Looks like I'll have to add the rest of you to the list."

"I'm not afraid of an angel." Jericho put his hand on his hip. "Least of all, a lone angel, who I'm assuming, has been cast out of heaven for this little stunt."

Sariel threw her head back and laughed. "That's where you wrong. I'm not alone."

Sariel motioned to a small golden dot that appeared next to her. The dot began to grow until it was the size of a door. Jericho and Alexander took a step back as they glared at the newly formed portal. A black combat boot stepped out first, belonging to Olaf Sader. Thaden stepped out next, carrying the Takara Dagger. They walked over and stood next to Sariel.

"You will find, Slayer," Sariel folded her arms. "That I'm never alone. It is my job to grant favors and receive them in return."

"Oh yeah?" Jericho smiled. "But I don't owe you a damn thing. So, what's gonna stop me from chopping off your head?"

"Even after our wild night," Sariel snapped fingers and transformed into Sarah. "I can't believe you'd ever want to hurt me or even lay one little finger on me."

"How's about a fist?" Tom leaped over Jericho's head and punched Sariel with his brass knuckles.

Sariel staggered to the side and grabbed her jaw. She'd transformed back into her angelic form

Tom recovered and turned to Jericho. "Jeez, Caine, you slept with this thing?"

Olaf pulled out his pistols and fired several shots.

Alexander held up his staff. "Vis ager (force field)."

The bullets bounced off a light blue field that surrounded Jericho, Tom, and Alexander.

Sariel turned to Olaf and Thaden and then pointed at the heroes. "Kill them! But the priest is mine."

"*You* don't give me orders, angel," Thaden said. "I will kill them, but because I want to, not because you're ordering me."

"Whatever, monster." Sariel stomped her foot. "Just do it."

Alexander pointed his staff at Olaf. "Lacus (Transport)."

A white beam of light-struck Olaf in the chest. It transported him and Alexander to the other side of the farm.

Thaden charged Jericho with his dagger out and swung. Jericho raised his sword and blocked the blade. They began a sword fight that moved quickly away from Sariel and Tom.

Tom and Sariel

"Now, Priest." Sariel washed her hands. "I'm going to do what Thaden and Ranken could not. You're a dead man."

Sariel held out her hand, and her sword appeared in it. She held it to her and head and nodded toward Tom. Tom held up his pole and got in his fighting stance. He clicked a button in the center, and sharp blades slid out.

Tom twirled the pole around in front of him and finally swung at Sariel's head. She blocked it with her sword and kicked Tom in the stomach. He backed up a few feet and positioned himself to strike again. She looked to the sky, and her eyes began to glow white. Suddenly her silver angelic armor slowly covered her body.

Tom frowned. "You need your armor for me? I'm just a puny human, remember?"

Sariel raised the faced guard of her helmet. "I think we both know that you more than that. Now prepare to die like the dog that you are."

Sariel jumped in the air and came down with her sword. Tom held up his pole to block it, but it was broken in half. He began swinging wildly at Sariel with both rods. She either blocked ducked, or moved out of the way of the attempted strikes. She kicked one of the broken poles out of Tom's hand and sent it sailing into the wheat field.

Tom continued his attack and backed up Sariel against a huge tree. He jabbed the other half of the pointed pole at her head. She moved to the side and popped Tom in the face with the handle of the sword. He staggered backward and tripped on a rock. He fell to the ground. Sariel walked over and stepped on the pole as Tom tried to raise it up. She then kicked it out of his hand, and it slid on the ground out of Tom's reach. She stomped on Tom's stomach with her metal boots, knocking the wind out of his body.

"So long, Priest," Sariel said as she raised her foot to stomp on Tom's head. "You should have chosen the hitman to fight."

Tom caught Sariel's foot as it came down toward his head. He tossed her foot to the side and spun her around. Tom quickly got to his feet and punched Sariel in the face with his brass knuckles. She fell forward and almost tumbled to the ground.

Tom got back in a fight stance. "I think I chose the right person."

"You dare believe you can defeat an angel." Sariel raised her sword in the attack position again. "What makes you think you are a match for me?"

"Simple. I'm a Death Brother. And you are a disgrace to all angels."

Sariel attacked again. She swung her sword like a baseball bat. Tom ducked as Sariel's momentum forced her off balance. Tom threw an uppercut. He connected to Sariel's jaw. Even wearing the metal helmet, she was knocked backward off her feet and landed on her back. Tom walked over to her. He couldn't see through the metal faceguard to see if she were conscious. He bent over to get a closer look and was met with a metal knee to his chest.

He was knocked backward through the air, bounced off the sandy gravel.

Alexander and Olaf

On another side of the field, Alexander and Olaf stared at each other. Alexander had his staff ready, and Olaf had his pistols in his hand. Alexander knew Olaf wasn't a threat to him. Besides being a deadly assassin, Olaf was still just a human. *There's no way he believes he a match for a Suma wizard.*

"I know you're supposed to be some big badass wizard," Olaf began. "But put down that little magic wand and fight me fair and square, like a man."

Alexander laughed. "Who said anything about being fair, assassin? But I'll humor you. I'll use a kendo stick, and you use whatever." He held out his free hand. "Kendo lignum unum (kendo stick)."

A kendo stick appeared in Alexander's hand. His staff then disappeared from the other. Once he looked back at Olaf, a loud bang sounded out, and a bullet grazed the side of Alexander's head. He dropped to the ground as blood dripped from the small gash on his head. His eyes were still open as the shock paralyzed him. He watched as Olaf approached with both guns pointed down at the wizard.

"That's what I love about you, good guys." Olaf smiled. "I never said, I was going to fight you fair and square. People like you just can't help themselves."

Olaf, surprisingly, holstered his pistols. He began to kick Alexander in the ribs. Alexander squirmed around on the ground in pain. He still couldn't move his limbs to defend himself. Olaf reached down and pulled out his knife from the ankle holster. He dropped to his knees next to Alexander's face.

"You will surely be the biggest kill of my life." Olaf licked the sharp side of his blade and grabbed Alexander by his hair. "I will be considered the best assassin in the world one this gets out."

Alexander began sweating as the vein in his forehead budged. He began to wiggle his toes. That let him knew that the shock was wearing off, and the feeling was returning to his body. *I just need a few more seconds, though. I need this idiot to keep talking.*

"O- Oh yeah?" Alexander managed to say. "G-Good f-for you."

Olaf pressed a finger into the wound on Alexander's head. "I must admit. I was nervous when I shot at you because I was aiming for the middle of your head. I rarely miss it. But now, I get to slit your throat instead. That makes this even sweeter."

Alexander wiggled his fingers and opened his hand. "C-C-Coward."

"Ha. Ha. Ha. Whatever." Olaf placed the blade to Alexander's throat. "I usually stay away from your supernatural type. Because let's face it, I'm just a regular guy. Guess it was only a matter of time, though."

Olaf began applying pressure with the knife against Alexander's throat. Alexander cut his eyes to the left hand and called his staff back to it. A burst of electricity erupted from the staff and covered both men. It forced Olaf to toss his knife to the side. He stood and staggered backward. He tried to reach for his pistols, but the electric current continued to surge and made his hands shake. As he was finally able to steady his hand and grab a gun, Olaf pointed the gun at Alexander. However, Alexander had disappeared.

"Where are you, wizard?" Olaf demanded. "Pish! And you called me a coward?"

Pop! Alexander's staff smashed into the back of Olaf's head. He fell face-first to the ground. He grazed the back of his head with his hand and then stared at his blood. He turned over and saw Alexander standing a few feet away. Alexander walked over and placed a foot on Olaf's chest to keep the assassin planted on the ground. Olaf raised his pistols.

"Not this time." Alexander waved his staff across the air. "Exarmaueris (Disarm)."

An invisible force snatched the pistols out of Olaf's hands. They hovered in front of Alexander. He then raised his staff to the sky, and the guns floated up until they were no longer visible. Olaf tried to kick Alexander in the groin, but the wizard simply knocked Olaf's leg away with his staff.

"You wouldn't kill an unarmed man, would you?" Olaf pleaded.

Alexander folded his arms while still holding his staff. "Do you remember how you said that you usually steer clear of us supernatural types? Well, you should have stayed away from this one too."

"Wait!" Olaf held up his hand at the reenergized wizard. "What if I promised to leave this country and never return?"

"You know what?" Alexander stroked his beard. "I can get on board with that idea. So, here's what we're gonna do. I'm going to call down lightning to this very spot. Your task is simple. All's you have to do is get out of the way before it hits, and I'll let you leave."

Olaf frowned. "That's it? Just move out of the way?"

"Yup."

"Fine."

Alexander took a step back. He looked up at the sky and then back to Olaf, who had a sinister smile on his face.

"Oh," Alexander began. "Did I forget to mention that you have to move this as well?" Alexander held up his staff. "Apparent scopulus (Boulder appear)."

Alexander turned to walk away. A huge rock appeared on Olaf's chest and stomach. He let out a huge breath as if he'd been punched in the gut. He tried to push the boulder away. Nothing. He tried to slide from underneath it. He couldn't.

"A-Are y-ou j-j-just going to l-leave me l-like this?" Olaf asked as sweat poured from his forehead.

Alexander turned back to Olaf. "Nope. I'm going to leave you like this." Alexander raised his staff toward the sky. "Fulgur (Lightning)!"

Alexander's eyes glowed white as a dark cloud hovered

above. Thunder erupted.

Olaf continued to struggle to get free. "P-Please, wizard. Please!"

"Goodbye, Mr. Sader."

Alexander walked away as he heard two lightning strikes pound the ground in the background. *Idiot shoots me in the head and thinks he gets a free pass. What's wrong with some people?*

Jericho and Thaden

"This is the way it should have been from the start." Thaden stared at Jericho and glided his hand across the Takara Dagger. "You have your sword, and I have the dagger."

"Really? Me killing you is what you thought was going to happen from the start?" Jericho smiled. "I'm flattered."

"I was told that you fancy yourself as some sort of comedian, Slayer." Thaden held out his free hand, and his sickle with a spiked metal ball appeared in it. "But death is the remedy for all humor."

Jericho nodded. "I couldn't agree more. I'll assume it's why you're not amused."

Thaden shot a golden beam of light from the dagger. He didn't wait to see the result, as he launched himself through the air at Jericho, swinging the spiked ball. Jericho blocked the beam of light with his sword, but the metal ball struck him in the chest. He staggered backward and clutched his chest. He saw there was no blood, so he charged Thaden and swung his sword. Thaden blocked it, and they commenced a back and forth duel. Thaden occasionally swung his sickle, but Jericho ducked or blocked those attempts.

Thaden kicked Jericho in the chest, catapulting he slayer backward. He flipped through the air and landed on his feet, and they charged each other again. However, Thaden flipped over Jericho's head and landed behind the slayer. Thaden pointed the dagger at Jericho's back and fired. The blast forced Jericho to drop the sword as it sent him flailing forward to the ground. He tried to push himself up, but Thaden kicked Jericho in the back of the head. Jericho's forehead crashed to the ground. He blinked in and out of consciousness.

"Goodbye, Slayer," Thaden said as he slowly raised the dagger to plunge it into Jericho's back. "I thought this would be a tougher fight."

Thaden plunged down with the dagger, and it was knocked away by Alexander's staff.

"Time for round three." Alexander rapidly raised his eyebrows. "What? You didn't really think I'd leave it at a draw, did you?"

"Wizard," Thaden said as he straightened. "I was gonna save you for last."

Jericho hunched over on all four limbs right behind Thaden. Alexander pointed his staff and fired an invisible pulse, striking Thaden in the chest. Thaden fell backward and fell over Jericho. Jericho, still on the ground as well, didn't wait for Thaden to recover as the slayer rolled over and repeatedly elbowed Thaden in the face and head.

Thaden's eyes rolled back and began to glow red. Fur covered the werewolf half of his body. Still, on the ground, Thaden reached over and grabbed Jericho by the throat with his werewolf hand. He flipped over and mounted the slayer. He punched Jericho in the face several times. Thaden then stood and pressed the slayer over his head. He tossed the Jericho to the side and summoned the Takara Dagger back to his hand.

Alexander swung his staff at Thaden's head, but the monster ducked. He spun around and back-kicked Alexander on the gunshot wound on the side of his head. Alexander dropped to one knee. Before he could get back to his feet, a golden beam of light trapped him in a forced field. Alexander clutched his throat and began to choke, as the air drained out of the force field. The force field floated a few feet off the ground, and Alexander dropped his staff.

Thaden walked over and stood face to face with Alexander. "There won't be a round four, wizard." Thaden cocked his head to the side and smiled. "I tried to tell you in New York, things are different now."

Jericho ran over and dropped kicked Thaden in the back. Thaden crashed into Alexander, which caused the field to disappear, and Alexander fell to the ground. The wizard coughed and gasped for air, while still clutching his throat.

Jericho looked around and saw his sword lying on the ground a few feet away. He held out his hand and called the sword back.

"You're getting ahead of yourself, wolf-boy." Jericho kicked Thaden in the stomach. "We haven't finished our round one yet."

"Funny," Sariel said as he ran over and punched Jericho in the face, sending him crashing into a tree. "I was just about to say the same thing. You didn't really think the priest would be able to take me, did you?"

Jericho checked the back of his head for blood. There was none, only ringing in his ears. He struggled to get up, and he fell back to his side. He looked around until he spotted Tom attempting to get back to his feet. Susie was still unconscious a few feet away, and Alexander was incapacitated. *Looks like we're taking a beating. I can't imagine what it would be like if we had to deal with the Hangman too.*

Suddenly, as if he had a burst of energy, Alexander rose to his feet. Jericho knew he had to act because the wizard had a look of determination in his eyes. Alexander stumbled over and grabbed Sariel's shoulder. She spun around and jammed her sword into Alexander's shoulder. She yanked out the sword, and he dropped to his knees. Blood spewed out of Alexander's shoulder and drenched his blue Chicago Cub's t-shirt. He grabbed his shoulder and Sariel pushed him to the ground. He tried to get up but sank back down.

"So that's it, wizard?" Jericho slowly crawled over to Alexander. "Are you just gonna quit?"

"Nobody's quitting, Caine," Alexander said. "I was just catching my breath."

"You should have stayed down." Sariel punched Jericho in the side of the head. "I'm through playing around with you guys.

Time to show you idiots who truly is in charge. Oof!"

Sariel's eyes widened. She turned around slowly as Thaden snatched his dagger out of her back. He smiled as he stared in her eyes as and she slumped down. She lay on her back, staring up at the sky. A golden glow surrounded her body. It flashed a few seconds. Her eyes rolled back, and her eyelids flickered. Thaden dropped to his knees and gripped his dagger with both hands. He raised it in the air and plunged it down into Sariel's chest. Her eyes glowed white for a few seconds and then closed. The golden glow covering her grew brighter and constant. Her body began to dissolve into a white foamy fluid until only her battle armor remained.

"Good riddance." Thaden got to one knee. "Only I will rule this world alone. I am in charge."

As Thaden stood, he was punched in the face. He staggered to the side and looked around to see where the fist originated. It was Jericho's massive fist. Thaden held his dagger over his head. A lightning bolt struck it, and an electric field engulfed his body. He pointed the blade at Jericho, and a stream of electricity flowed from it and blasted him. The slayer sailed backward and smacked the back of his head on the ground as he landed a few feet away. *This is getting old.*

Thaden then turned his attention to Alexander and slowly walked toward him. "Bye, bye, wizard. You should have stayed out of this fight."

Alexander looked around and spotted Susie unconscious

body. Alexander yelled out in pain as he struggled to get back to his feet.

"You know what, Thaden? You're right." Alexander pointed his staff at Susie. "Lanuae magicae (teleport)."

He disappeared through a portal and reappeared next Susie. He reached down, picked up Susie, and placed her over his shoulder. As he was about to step back into the portal, a golden beam of light struck him in the chest. Alexander dropped to his knees and almost dropped Susie. He glared up at Thaden, who walked toward the wounded wizard.

Thaden pointed his dagger at Alexander again. "You're out of tricks, wizard. No one can survive another shot from the dagger."

Tom dove through the air and punched Thaden in the back of the head, sending the creature tumbling hard to the ground.

"Guess that means it's my turn." Tom turned and waved his hand at Alexander. "Go ahead, Alexander. Take her and get out of here."

Alexander, still glowing, rose to his feet with Susie still draped across his shoulder. "Don't worry, Thomas," Alexander said. "I'll take care of her. Then I'll come and find you."

"No." Tom shook his head. "The Hangman is gone. You're done here. Thank you, my friend."

The golden glow surrounding Alexander's body dissipated. He nodded at Tom and walked slowly through the portal.

As the portal closed, Dr. Ranken stepped forward, holding a gun, and pointed it at Tom. "I thought he'd never leave. It's just you and me now. My vengeance is at hand."

Suddenly, the Sword of Caine plunged through Dr. Ranken's chest. He turned around to see Jericho approaching. He fell to his knees, reached behind his back, and tried to pull out the sword. He couldn't.

"S-Slayer." Dr. Ranken managed to say. "Y-Y-You won't w-win."

Dr. Ranken fell to his side and died. Jericho walked over and pulled his sword from the doctor's back.

Jericho turned to Tom. "I didn't even know who he was, but I'm sure the world's better off without him. Jericho reached out his hand. "Oh, crap! Duck, Priest!?"

Tom ducked with no hesitation, just in time to avoid being beheaded by Thaden's dagger. Tom rolled on the ground and got back to his feet.

Thaden glanced at Dr. Ranken's body and then back to Jericho. "You've killed my sisters, and now, my creator. You two will pay for that."

Jericho walked over and stood next to Tom. He reached down

into oversized pockets on the side of his pants. He pulled out a short steel pole. It's was Tom's older and backup pole. He handed it to Tom, who stretched it out until sharp knives appeared at both ends. Tom then reached over his head and pulled off his brown beaded necklace and let the crucifix hang.

Thaden held out his hand, and his sickle appeared in it. "So, this is where this generation's Death Brother meet their end?"

"I can't tell if people really mean that when they say it." Jericho glanced at Tom. "But since we're still here, I'm pretty sure it's just something people need to say."

Tom smiled. "Frankly, I'm actually tired of hearing it."

"I'm gonna kill Caine." Jericho mocked. "I'm gonna kill Padilla. Give it a rest for crying out loud."

"Funny till the end, eh guys?" Thaden smiled and nodded. "Well, there's only one way to end it."

Thaden swung the metal ball at Jericho, who ducked and tried to come back up with an uppercut, but Thaden moved to the side to avoid it. He had to sidestep just as quickly as the knife from Tom's pole almost struck him in the chest. Thaden's canine teeth appeared. He leaped into the air and come down on top of Tom. He punched Tom in the jaw twice before Jericho's huge boot kicked the creature in the face. Thaden rolled over on the ground; when he sat up, he shot a gold beam of light at Jericho. Jericho blocked it with his sword.

Jericho held his sword in the air. A bolt of lightning struck the sword and electrified it. Jericho then pointed the sword at Thaden. Electricity flowed from the Sword of Caine and zapped Thaden. His body convulsed as the electric current ravaged through it.

"You smell that, Tom?" Jericho laughed. "Smells like burnt dog around here."

Tom covered his nose. "It wreaks."

Thaden squirmed around the ground. He rolled over and grabbed Tom's leg. The electric current then flowed through Tom's body as well.

Jericho rushed over and kicked Thaden's hand away from Tom's leg. The electric current stopped.

"Dammit, Caine!" Tom bent to one knee. "Really?"

"Sorry, Priest." Jericho pulled Tom back to his feet. "I didn't expect him to do that."

Thaden, from a seated position, swung and hit Jericho in the stomach with the spiked metal ball. "You probably didn't expect that either, Slayer."

Thaden jumped to his feet, shot a gold beam of light from his dagger, and struck the bent over slayer in the head. Jericho hurled backward and crash-landed on the front porch of the old house, while his sword went crashing through the window. He struggled to get back to his feet, but he could only crawl back toward Tom and Thaden.

Thaden placed the dagger in his pants in the small of his back. "Let's see what you've got, Priest."

Tom didn't hesitate as he swung his beads and popped Thaden in the side of the head. The silver crucifix left a welt on the creature. Thaden's canine teeth disappeared, replaced by his vampire's teeth.

"Enough of this," Thaden said as he pulled out his dagger again. "That's my lesson for trying to fight fair. But now, I think I'll have to go with our original plan to break up you two."

Thaden held out the dagger. It glowed bright gold, and he disappeared in the cloud of golden mist. He reappeared behind Tom and sliced the priest's shoulder with the dagger. Tom clutched his wound and spun quickly, swinging his pole, but Thaden had disappeared in a golden cloud again. He reappeared behind Jericho, who had almost crawled back over to the fight. Thaden swung the metal ball and struck Jericho the back of his head. Thaden disappeared again as the slayer fell face first with blood streaming from his head. Jericho's bloodied blonde hair was almost completely red, as he put fingers to his forehead and tried to focus.

Jericho's nose began to bleed as he looked up at Tom. *This guy isn't playing anymore. We've gotta come up with a plan and get that dagger away from him.*

Thaden appeared behind Tom and grabbed the priest in a headlock with his werewolf arm. "I'm going to do something *worse* than killing you, Padilla. I'm going to turn you into a vampire and see how your relationship with the slayer fairs after that."

Thaden reared his head back, and his vampire's teeth grew longer. He forced Tom's head to the side to expose his neck.

Jericho, too weak to stand, held out his hand. "Nooo!"

Thaden bit down into Tom's jugular vein. Before he could begin a suck Tom's blood, Tom shoved his sharpened pole through Thaden's foot. Thaden screamed out, and Tom elbowed him in the stomach, releasing Thaden's arm from around his neck. Tom then turned and stabbed Thaden in the heart with his pole. Thaden's eyes grew wider as he stepped a few feet backward. He grabbed the bar and pulled it out of his chest. He dropped to his knees and lowered his head.

Tom slowly walked over and picked up his pole again. He positioned it to stab Thaden again, but the creature didn't move. Tom turned to Jericho, who nodded with a smile on his face. That was until he heard faint laughter. When he turned around to face Thaden, the only thing remaining was a cloud of golden mist.

"Are you really that dumb, Priest?" A voice echoed in the open field. "I thought you were supposed to be smart. I don't have a vampire heart anymore. I can't be killed that way."

Tom began looking all around. "Oh, crap!"

"Oh, crap is right." Thaden appeared from behind Tom and blasted him with a beam of golden light. "You both are done."

"Thomas!" Jericho yelled from across the way.

Tom's body glowed as he lay flat on his stomach and began to crawl toward Jericho. Blood raced from his nose, and sweat poured from his head. Jericho began to crawl as well. Surprisingly, Tom stopped crawling. He stared up into the air and sighed. He pressed his two fingers against his temple and stared at Jericho. Both of their noses began to bleed as Tom reached out telepathically.

I'm going to do for us what you once did for me. Tom's eyes became bloodshot. *We'll only get one chance at this. I just hope you'll know what to do…after.*

"Wait, Tom." Jericho shook his head. "What are you talking about?"

Let me get up first, big guy. Trust me.

Tom yelled out in pain and used his remaining strength to get back to his feet. Thaden reappeared and stood in the middle of Tom and Jericho. The creature studied both men and decided to attack slayer.

"If that was all you've got," Tom began as the golden glow disappeared from around his body. "No wonder you're going to

212

lose."

Thaden turned to Tom. "Thanks for changing my mind on who to kill first, Priest."

Oh, shit, Thomas. It finally dawned on Jericho what Tom meant. Jericho scanned the area, closed his eyes, and held out his hand. Thaden walked over to Tom and stared in the priest's face. Tom put up his fists, and Thaden quickly knocked Tom's arms back down. Tom's knees shook, and he almost fell forward. He was spent.

Thaden grabbed Tom's shoulder and then rammed the Takara Dagger into Tom's chest. Thaden pulled out the dagger and let Tom's lifeless body fall to the ground. Thaden erupted in laughter. However, his blade began to glow and heat up. He grunted and attempted to turn around, but it was too late. The Sword of Caine, glowing bright white, sliced through Thaden's neck and chopped off his head. The vampire half of Thaden's body, along with his head, burst into fiery ashes. The werewolf half-collapsed to the ground, along with the Takara Dagger.

Jericho frowned. "Gross!"

Jericho stuck his sword into the ground and bent over to rest his hands on his knees. He then realized that Tom had been stabbed. He looked up and rushed over to Tom's body. He turned Tom flat on his back and slapped him gently on the face.

"Come on, Priest." Jericho sat and rested Tom's head on his lap. "Don't do this to me. We're a team, dammit. Priest! Priest!"

Jericho shook Tom's shoulders, but nothing happened. Tears welled up in his eyes. He'd lost assistants in the past, but this was different.

"Please, Tom. Please wake up. You can't die on me."

Jericho looked up and around the sky as he heard wings fluttering. He shook his head and refocused on Tom. There was nothing more important. He didn't drop Tom's head or budge. He didn't care what was happening until he looked up again and saw the seven-foot angel, Arellos, staring down at him.

"Did you come to rub it in?" Jericho asked. "Now's not the time, angel."

"Believe it or not, Slayer," Arellos began. "Heaven remains you guys biggest fans. I'm here to help. But you're gonna have to do something that you haven't wanted to do in a long time."

"Oh yeah?" Jericho wiped the tears from his eyes. "And what's that?"

"You're gonna have to believe again, Caine."

Jericho looked down at Tom again and remembered what Tom said right before he was stabbed. *I'm going to do for us what you once did for me.* The message had become clearer. Jericho had dived in front of Tom and was stabbed in the back by the demon, known as Pick. Jericho was dead. Tom placed his hands on Jericho using one of their abilities and prayed to bring back the slayer. It was now Jericho's turn, but he didn't want to pray. He'd given up hope on the angels and Heaven, but he knew Tom believed, and that was enough. So, he had to try.

Jericho placed his hand on the bloody wound on Tom's chest. He closed his eyes. *I know I'm not a believer, but please, Tom is my friend, my brother. Please bring him back.* Nothing happened. He looked down at Tom and then up at Arellos, who simply hunched his shoulders.

"So, is this my punishment for years of not believing?" Jericho asked.

"You've got to go deeper, Slayer." Arellos bent down to one knee. "You're the only one that can do this. Dig deeper. Find that inner peace and even anger that binds you two together."

Jericho closed his eyes again. He let his mind drift to old memories of him and Tom. He remembered when he first met Tom at the house in Brooklyn, when they took down Tobias' nest; he remembered when he, Tom, BA, and the Hangman fought side by side in the Nevada desert; how Tom always stepped in to stop his squabbles with BA; when Tom, BA, and Alexander showed up to help him defeat the vampire angel Dakota; and finally when Tom prayed to bring him back to life in the alley behind the church.

Jericho's breathing slowed. *Please, Tom. There is good in this world, whether it's from angels or people like you. I love you. And I couldn't have done any of it without you, brother.*

Jericho opened one of his eyes and looked around. Nothing was happening. He sensed Arellos still looking on: Jericho sighed and was about to give up. However, the sky darkened. Thunder and lightning rang out in the sky as energy flowed through Jericho's body and into Tom. It was a numbing sensation. Jericho looked up at Arellos, who was nodding and smiling.

"Not a traditional prayer," Arellos said. "But for you, Slayer, looks like it will do."

Tom's eyes opened, and electricity pulsated from them. He coughed several times and reached up the grab Jericho's hand. A smile appeared on Jericho's face as well. He looked down at Tom's wound, which had healed. The energy stopped as they glared at each other.

"You did it, my friend," Tom said. "My brother. You did it. I didn't really think the whole plan through, but I hoped this is what would happen."

"You scared me, Priest." Jericho helped Tom sit up. "Don't ever do that again."

Tom looked up at Arellos and nodded. "I see you had some help, though."

Jericho folded his arms and groaned. "Well, seeing as this

whole situation was caused by an angel, it was the least that they could do."

"Looks like things are back to normal around here." Arellos shook his head. "Good to have you back, Thomas." He sprouted his wings and nodded at Jericho, "Slayer."

Arellos took off as Jericho and Tom stood and watched until the angel was out of sight.

"What now?" Tom asked.

"Well, I need to make funeral arrangements for my mother." Jericho patted Tom on the back. "And you have a girlfriend to go catch up with. Maybe, even a little sex."

Tom chuckled. "Jesus, Caine. You have no filter. But there are some things that make this life we've chosen worthwhile."

"Indeed." Jericho sheathed his sword. "By the way, let Ms. Taki know that my offer still stands."

Tom frowned but smiled. "Um…ok. But I don't know if I like the sound of that."

"She'll know what I'm talking about." Jericho then let out a deep sigh. "And don't forget. We still have a pissed off Hangman out there, somewhere, to deal with."

"Don't remind me."

The End

www.ingramcontent.com/pod-product-compliance
Lightning Source LLC
Chambersburg PA
CBHW060640260626
47161CB00008B/2932